TWIN TURMOIL

VANESSA BROOKS

Published by Blushing Books
An Imprint of
ABCD Graphics and Design, Inc.
A Virginia Corporation
977 Seminole Trail #233
Charlottesville, VA 22901

Brooks, Vanessa
Twin Turmoil

eBook ISBN: 978-1-62750-926-8
Print ISBN: 978-1-64563-132-3
v1

Cover Art by ABCD Graphics & Design
This book contains fantasy themes appropriate for mature readers only. Nothing in this book should be interpreted as Blushing Books' or the author's advocating any non-consensual sexual activity.

For my friend Annie

Prologue

Josie Carter tossed the cardboard box onto her sofa and kicked off her shoes. Padding barefoot around the breakfast bar into the kitchen area, she opened her fridge and grabbed a diet coke. Before she could open it, her mobile chirruped and she set the ice-cold can down on the kitchen counter and read the text. *Have you decided yet?* It was from her boyfriend, Max. She texted him back: *No, you said I had until Friday!*

Josie wandered back into the living room and realized that the box she had launched at the sofa had bottomed out and the contents were spilling everywhere. She sighed and went to retrieve a heavy crystal vase that had probably been the cause of the collapse due to its weight. It had been her mother's favorite vase. Her English great-grandmother, Susan St. Clare, had given it to Josie's mom as part of her mother's wedding gift when Josie's parents had married. She picked up the vase and set it on the counter, out of harm's way. The vase didn't quite fit in with Josie's minimalist décor, but she wanted to keep it as a reminder of her departed mother.

Josie's mother had died two years ago from bowel cancer. It

had been a terrible time for all the family, especially for her father. Josie was pleased that he had sold the family home near San Diego and bought himself a condo. The new place was a much better fit for him as he was nearer to the golf course where he practically lived nowadays. Visiting the family home had been a painful reminder to Josie that Mom had gone; salt in the wound as she used to say.

So Josie had been there today helping her Dad make the new condo homey and he had given her a box of Mom's memorabilia to take home with her.

Still sipping from the can of coke, Josie pushed the box along the sofa and sat beside it, delving into it randomly with her free hand. She lifted out her Mom's old year book from school and flicked through it briefly before setting it aside and digging into the box again. This time she brought out an old hard backed writing pad. Josie flicked it open; it seemed to be some kind of diary but not in her mother's handwriting. Setting the coke down on the floor next to the sofa, she flicked open the book to the first page. Her Grandmother Nicola's diaries... wow! Why did her Mom have this?

Josie's grandparents were both psychology experts, specializing in working with teenagers. They had run a boot camp for wayward teens on their ranch in California for years. Three years ago, they had retired and moved to Corbin's Bend. The community was located near Denver, where Josie's grandfather had grown up.

Because Josie's mother had been diagnosed with cancer at about that time, Josie had never visited their new home. There had been no time for visiting once her mother had become terminally ill. Her Grandmother Nicola had come and stayed with them, nursing her dying daughter with love and deep sorrow, all the while giving comfort and support.

After her Mom's funeral, Josie's grandparents had encouraged her to get on with her own life, to finish her education and training as a nurse. They offered their home to Josie as a safety net, any time Josie should need their love and support. So far she hadn't the time to visit them in Colorado.

Settling herself comfortably against the cushions, Josie began to read.

1967

TO EXORCISE *my ghosts I have written my story down. Perhaps someday my children and grandchildren will want to read my tale but for now this is just for me, to help me process the trauma of my recent past.*

1

Shock

I struggled to get the key into the lock. It was no easy task with my arms full of shopping bags and wet hair dripping into my eyes. Swearing gently under my breath, I stabbed at the lock and at last the door swung inwards. As I stumbled inside, I caught sight of myself reflected in the hall mirror, and I stuck out my tongue at the bedraggled apparition. "So much for capable and well groomed," I muttered with disgust; the cold March day had done its worst.

It was proving more difficult than I had thought, pursuing a career in the world of publishing. I had to maintain the highest standards of appearance if I was to compete with my male colleagues. Although I was hopeful that one day I would be a full-fledged editor, I was at present a sub-editor in a small publishing house that dealt with mainly medical publications. Publishing was a hard industry to break into as a woman, even with a first class degree in English Literature.

Dumping the groceries bags onto the table in the hallway, I made my way through to my bedroom while flicking through the handful of mail I had retrieved on my way inside. Bills, bills....

and, yes... more bills. I threw the offending letters onto the bed and, shivering violently now, quickly stripped off my wet clothes. In the bathroom, I turned on the bath taps and filled the tub with steaming hot water.

Climbing in, I leaned against the back of the bathtub and sighed. Closing my eyes, I let the heat soothe and warm me as images of my horrible day passed across my closed lids. Unusually clumsy, I had started the morning badly by spilling my precious early tea all over today's copy. Strangely, I had felt emotional and close to tears all day, yet my period wasn't due for another fortnight or so. I always got emotional and weepy just before a period, whereas my mother always seemed to sail through hers without a hiccup—typical. "Don't go there!" I spoke aloud. The last person I wanted to think about after the horrible day I had just endured was my dearest mama.

A foul and disjointed day it had been, but it was behind me now, and I gradually eased and let the stress drain away. I gave myself up to pure physical relaxation, contemplating with pleasure an evening at home in front of the newly acquired television set, perhaps even one of the first colour television sets in my apartment building. How cool was that?

The simple chore of preparing my supper soothed my rattled nerves. I carried my meal through to the sitting room and switched on the electric fire. Wearing my bathrobe, I sat down with a bowl of steaming tomato soup and crackers balanced on my knees. After turning on the television set, I took a few spoonfuls of soup while I waited for the television to warm up. When it finally came into focus, I froze, paralysed by the unbelievable sight of an image of *my face* filling the small bulbous television screen. My tray slipped unnoticed to the floor, while I jumped up and fumbled uselessly with the knobs on the set frantically trying to turn up the sound. By the time I managed to do so, the piece ended and the reporter had moved on to the next news item.

A repetitive ringing penetrated my brain, drowning out the sound of the television, which now blared out something about the forthcoming London political elections. Then it dawned on me, the noise—it was the telephone! I stumbled on the discarded tray, slipping and burning my bare foot in the hot soup. Muttering crossly, I managed to reach the phone and grab it, "Chelsea, two, four, one," I bellowed above the now blaring television.

"Darling, you're home!"

"Mother?"

"Look," she interrupted. 'I assume you've seen the news?"

"Yeah—"

"Darling listen, I don't want you to worry. I'm going to send Jenkins over with the Rolls because I want you to come and stay here tonight."

"Mother do you know anything about this? What is going on? How did you pull this one off? The news—the photograph it was—*me!"*

"Look, Nicola darling, I cannot talk to you about this over the telephone. Just come here a.s.a.p. please."

"Come on, Mother, out with it. Did you give them my photograph? What is going on... is this some kind of a hoax? Because I can tell you now that I am not amused!"

"Please, Nicky… there are… things. Oh dear, I must *see* you… *talk* to you. I can't do this over the telephone. Just throw some bits and bobs into a bag and Jenkins will be there shortly. Nicky? Nicola? Do you hear me? Are you still there, darling?"

"What the *hell* is going on, Mother?"

"I left several messages at your firm today asking you to contact me."

Yes, I know, and I ignored them all, just as I always do when I am at work. I knew from past experience what sort of trivia my mother considered important. I dragged a hand through my damp hair. I didn't know what to think. My blasted mother, what had she done now?

Knowing from past experience that I would get nowhere questioning her over the telephone, I acquiesced.

"I'll be with you shortly… oh, and, Mother?"

"Yes, dear?"

"This had better be good!"

I slammed down the phone and wrapped my arms around myself, shut my eyes and shuddered. All day I had felt off-key, sort of unbalanced with an overpowering sense of impending doom. What was this piece about me on the news and how had they gotten hold of a photograph of me? Mother perhaps was trying to impress some friend or other, but it seemed incredible and unlikely that a news researcher had allowed some sort of practical joke. I hurried into my bedroom to pack an overnight bag.

After the short drive to my mother's house, Jenkins carried my holdall up the steps and into the hall; I knew that insisting that I carry my own bag was a complete waste of breath. Jenkins had been with my mother for the last fifteen years. He was a gentle, shy Welsh man with a will of iron and a heart of butter. He adored my silly mother. He was happily married to my mother's housekeeper-cook, Dilys. Between them, the pair cosseted and spoiled my selfish and infuriating mother. She, in return for their loyalty, bought them a cottage in Wales so that they could be near their family. They spent holidays and the odd weekend up there, generally when my mother was away herself. The plan was to retire there together, but I privately think it unlikely that they will ever leave my mother, so devoted are they to her. However, I hope they will because they deserve time to themselves after the years spent chasing around after the extremely demanding Susan St. Clare.

Knowing that my mother would be in her drawing room, I headed up the stairs. Out of habit, I tapped lightly on the door before entering. She called out, her voice wavering slightly, "Nicola is that you, darling? Come in, do."

Standing before the fake log fire was my mother. Her slight, straight body was clothed in black and her perfectly made up face looked pale. From the doorway, I could see that she had been crying. "Mother, are you feeling quite all right... whatever is wrong?" My anger towards her dissipated with concern; she *never* cried. Quickly, I crossed the room and hugged her small frame. She allowed me that brief contact, even leaning into me slightly before stepping deftly away.

"Sit down, Nicola, please, what I have to tell you won't be easy for either of us." I did as she asked, taking a seat next to the fire, grateful on this occasion for the overly warm room and comforting blaze. My mother stood and smoothed her hands nervously down her Jaeger skirted hips. She stood turned away from me as she began to talk in a low voice. I felt uneasy at her obvious distress as my mother was normally always so very sure of herself. This behaviour was not like her at all.

After a few false starts, she began again in that strained voice. "I married very young you see, very rashly in a whirlwind of romance. Not a suitable man, my father said, and that was putting it rather politely."

"Not cool, Mother. I know all this, please just tell me why my picture was on the news bulletin tonight!"

"Nicola, please be patient. I have to tell you the whole story. Just listen please and stop interrupting me. Where was I? Ah yes, your father. He was a bear of a man—a veritable giant—larger than life in every way. In his laugh, his capacity for joy, his gargantuan appetite, oh how that man could eat and make… hmm, anyway, he had tremendous drive and energy." She fell silent, lost in thought.

Confused, I waited. As far as I knew, my father had never been described thus before. He was rarely mentioned while I was growing up. I had assumed his death had been a huge blow to my mother, one that meant she could not bring herself to mention his name due to the weight of her grief. As I grew older,

I refrained from asking questions about him out of consideration for her feelings. When I was about six-years-old, my maternal grandparents had died in a car accident while on holiday on the continent. Thus, I had no close family to question about my father. I had been told that his parents had died before I was born.

Suddenly, she swung around to face me and looked at me with such a strange and wistful expression. "Forgive me, Nicola," she pleaded softly. Alarmed, I stood up but she shook her head at me and flapped her hand, indicating that I should stay where I was. I lowered myself back into the chair.

"Mother, you must tell me what the matter is. I can't help you unless you tell me what is wrong."

She walked over and lifted her hand to my cheek, resting it there in an uncharacteristic caress. "My darling, I have lied to you... oh for the very best of intentions, but I have lied nonetheless. I do hope you will understand that when I explain to you…"

"Explain what? Just tell me, Mother!"

Taking a deep breath and straightening up, she said, "Your father is *not* dead, Nicola. He is very much alive and is on his way over from the United States to meet with you." I stared at her in shock. My father *alive*... on his way to meet me? How and... why?

I realised that I was standing beside the fireside chair with no recollection of moving there. My mother walked to the drinks table and poured me a drink. When she handed me a glass of scotch, I took it gratefully even though I only usually drank wine. I took comfort from a mouthful of umber liquid which warmed me through.

"Nicky there is more… but first let me tell you that I love you more than anyone in the world and that I would not deliberately hurt you for anything. Nicola?"

I roused myself and stared at her, was this the mother I

thought I knew so well? I shivered. "What is his name—*my father*?" I asked, my voice shaking.

"Carl Keedon."

"Not the motel millionaire?" Keedon Motels were situated in every state of America; the distinctive C.K. interwoven logo a familiar sight to travellers. The appeal was universal, people knew what to expect from a Keedon motel. Each room was decorated in the same way using the same colour scheme. The menu offered the same choices whether you were in California or New Hampshire. The quality was consistently good and affordable. It was a new idea, a motel chain identical in every way, throughout every state. It was a highly profitable venture that had turned Carl Keedon into a millionaire.

My mother continued. "That's right. Carl and I met at the Torrington's end-of-war celebration party. As soon as I saw Carl, I knew I had to have him. Today, we would have simply had a torrid affair and gone our separate ways, but our parents were such a strong influence on both of us, and so we were married. We lived on his parents' ranch in Arizona and, at first, everything was fine. At that time, he was at the very beginning of his business venture. I travelled with him whenever he was away on business trips investigating suitable locations to build his motels. Then a year after our marriage, I discovered that I was pregnant. Carl was an old-fashioned sort, pig headed and stubborn; he stopped me travelling with him. I was to stay on the ranch with his mother. Well, you know me, darling, I need people, not cows, and I became lonely and bored. I would have followed him on his travels regardless, except that the doctor discovered… something… rather unusual about my pregnancy."

She faltered and reached for her drink, and to my amazement, she downed her glass of scotch in one swallow. She carefully replaced the glass on the small table. "You see, darling, I was expecting twins and I had to rest all the time." She stopped speaking and looked at me. I stared back at her not allowing any thought into my mind—I didn't dare to think.

"Go on," I said softly.

"Ellie, Carl's mother, your grandmother, was ill at that time, lung cancer. Shortly after the babies were born, she died. I was very depressed and so very unhappy. The marriage had been a mistake; we had nothing in common and I was so very homesick. I tried, Nicola, I really did. Then I found out that your father was having an affair, and I decided to leave, but he wouldn't let me take my babies! He said he loved you both too much. He was a good father; I have to admit that. He doted on you both, adored you, actually I was even jealous… yes, of my own daughters!"

"Daughters, plural?" I queried dully, *for I knew*, deep in my soul I had always known.

"Yes, Nicola, you and your twin… your sister, Claire."

She carried on talking trying to justify what she and my father had done. We looked alike, and so they each took one of us and felt it was a good compromise. I sat heavy with silent horror.

I had seen the 1961 film *The Parent Trap*. It had starred the actress Hayley Mills—she had played both of the twins in the film. Separated as babies, each parent had taken a twin and raised her, without either of the girls realising that they had a twin sister. In a chance encounter at a summer camp, the twins realise they are sisters and work out what their parents have done. Each twin swap places with the other, so that they could each meet the other parent. The film ends happily with the parents reunited and the family together once more.

My mother knew that I had been fascinated by that film. I had talked about it for some time afterwards; I even asked her if I had a twin living somewhere since the story in the film had got under my skin in such a peculiar way. She had laughed, teasing me about liking such a childish film. Over the years, I have thought about that film many times, always with a deep and unexplained longing.

As I sat in the overheated room, my skin prickled and burned. Inside me, anger steamed and rose up like molten lava, filling me, bubbling and boiling, desperate for release. With a rush of uncontrolled rage, I leapt forward and slapped her silly, selfish, face.

"How could you!" I said, hissing with rage, pushing my face into hers, this woman, my mother, whom I had trusted had betrayed me. She had betrayed my twin, and she had denied me the right of a father, a sister, a twin sister. Oh God, a *twin sister*! All fluent command of the English language deserted me; I was speechless with disbelief and absolute fury.

A sudden terrible thought jumped into my mind. "The face on the news, tell me…" Her face had already been pale but now was white. She shook her head, and a tear rolled down her face.

But of course I knew.

Hadn't I felt it all day?

I was the Sycamore seed that would no longer spin joyously in the autumn breeze, for I had lost my other half, and I fell sickeningly to the ground. Suddenly, I felt so alone. My mouth was dry, and I felt desperate. The vitriol poured out of me in a vicious torrent bursting forth towards my mother.

"I asked you if I had a twin!" I think I was screaming at her, so wild and livid was I—so hurt. "You lied about my father… lied about my twin! You… utterly… deceitful… bitch! When I think…"

"Stop right there! I'd say that will just about do. Not-one-more-word-comes out of your mouth, young lady—not if you know what's good for you!"

I spun around in shocked surprise at the sound of the man's voice booming into the room. A large man, with a shock of salt-and-pepper hair, was standing on the threshold of the drawing room. My impression was of a man with a heavy jaw line and deep craggy face; his eyes were the deepest blue.

"If you want to blame anyone, Nicola, then blame me. Blame…" he paused and stared intently at me, "*your father.*"

I stiffened, rigid with shock, unable to speak. He moved swiftly for a large man and caught me as I swayed. The blessed darkness washed over me, ending for a while at least, the horror of it all.

2

Disbelief

We talked later when I had rested. He came into what had been my childhood room, bringing me a cup of tea, like any other father would do for his sick child. I marvelled that he was there, sitting on the couch watching me as I sipped the fragrant brew. I longed to touch him, for him to hold me, the child within me needy. Perhaps I felt this keenly because I had been denied his love and support as a child.

He spoke and I listened in wonder to his deep and rolling voice.

I don't believe this, I thought. This is my father. It really is—*my father!*

"I have seen you periodically over the years, Nicky. Watched you as you were growing up." I looked up at him astonished. He nodded. "Oh yes, when you played Ariel in the school play, I was in the audience. When you played hockey in that tournament in Holland, I was there, standing at the back of the crowd cheering you on. Your graduation was the last time I saw you. You have grown into a very lovely young woman, Nicola." I lowered my eyes and took a sip of tea to cover my emotional confusion.

"Why have you come now? I mean… why wait until now to

see me? I needed you as a child and you weren't there for me then, so I wonder… why now?"

He frowned and nodded slowly. "All I can tell you is this, Nicky. I have never stopped loving you, and I want you to know that. I have no excuses for what I did. I thought I was right but now… I just don't know." He ran a hand over his face. I noticed how haggard he looked, how exhausted.

"I am here now because Claire, your sister, has been," he hesitated and his voice shook when he spoke, "murdered."

"*Murdered?*" I put my cup down with a clatter. "The television —my, *no, her face…*"

"Yup," he said, shuddering. His face was taut with grief and I saw tears well in his blue eyes. My mother's were hazel, so I had my father's eyes; it was a small comfort to me for some strange reason.

I glanced away, embarrassed by such raw and private emotion. He recovered himself, straightened, drew out a large blue handkerchief, and blew his nose with a blast.

"What happened and why was she… killed?" I asked, hesitantly.

"As to that, I really don't know why. She was found on Pinto Rock some six miles from The Plomosa ranch where we live. Claire had been strangled and her horse was discovered nearby."

"Oh my God, no!" I was so shocked that I didn't know what else to say. My own twin murdered. The pain of that knowledge was like a physical blow. It hurt me even to draw breath.

"Are the police looking for the killer? Do they have any idea of who did this?"

"Nope, they've no idea at all." He took a shuddering breath. A silence descended as we both fell into our separate reveries.

"What was Claire like… my twin?" I asked softly. My chest was knotted with pain due to a single thought that now I would never know her. My father—how strange that sounded—stretched out his large hand and tucked a strand of my long hair behind my ear. He stroked his knuckles down my cheek with paternal gentleness.

"She wore her hair tucked behind her ears, it was a little longer than your hair and maybe a slightly lighter shade of brown due to all the sunshine. She was your absolute double, Nicola, your identical twin." He sat quietly watching me as I digested this eerie information. I jumped when he spoke again, so deeply lost in thought had I been.

"Claire was gentle, sweet natured and kind. She loved horses, well, all animals really, but especially horses. She didn't develop academically the way you have. Oh, don't misunderstand me, she was bright, a real wizard with figures, but she was extremely miserable when she was away from home. She just loved the ranch. She chose to attend a college nearby so she could still stay at home on the ranch." He stopped speaking with a grimace. I noticed a tear slip down his cheek and absently, he withdrew the blue handkerchief and mopped his eyes.

A surprising stab of jealousy shot through me at his obvious love for his daughter, my unknown twin Claire. I had spent my school years at boarding school, often spending the holidays at the Jenkins' place in Wales, while my mother spent time gadding about Europe in a social whirl. I was ashamed that I should feel so jealous of my own sister—my d*ead* sister, I reminded myself and shivered.

My father was now deep in thought, so I coughed politely to draw his attention back to the present.

"You said that she was found on the ranch?" I prompted gently.

"Yeah, as I said, she was found at Pinto Rock. The police think she was throttled. She had gone for an early morning ride and when she didn't return, Matt rode out to look for her. He found her, the poor guy."

"Matt?" I queried.

"Huh? Oh right, yeah, Matthew Lane, he was sweet on Claire and they kind of had an understanding."

"Yes I see, but who is he?" I asked.

"Oh, hon', I'm real sorry, I forget you don't know anyone at home do you?" He looked concerned and I felt uncomfortable, it seemed an odd emphasis.

"No, after all it's *not* my home, thanks to you and my mother," I said, sharply.

He stood up abruptly. "Look, Nicky, I'm tired after the flight and I need to speak with Susan, your mother. Don't be too hard on her, honey, she has lost one daughter and she won't want to lose another."

I made a derisive noise in the back of my throat.

"You are still in shock. Come to that, so am I… but it is painful to look at you wearing Claire's face, knowing that she is… why don't we call it a night and I'll see you in the morning. I'm staying at the Ritz. Please come join me for breakfast. Would eight thirty be okay?"

Well, what could I say?

My father had just returned from the dead and I was hungry for information, for any crumb of detail about him or my sister.

"Yeah, cool… tomorrow then. Um, goodnight… Father."

He bent and kissed me and was gone. I lay back on the pillows and tried to make some sense of it all.

THE WAITER MOPPED up the tea from the table at the Ritz where I had dropped my tea cup just seconds before. He clicked his fingers for another tablecloth to be bought over. I sat oblivious to this. I was flabbergasted; how many more shocks were there in store for me I wondered?

My father thanked the waiter, who gave a slight bow while catching my eye. He did not smile but managed to convey, with stiff politeness, his utter disapproval of me. This was done in such a clever way. He had perfected the art of conveying disgust, all wrapped up with superior politeness. My father, seemingly unaware of the mishap, continued to talk.

"The police would know your real identity, of course, but on the ranch, only Matt and I will know your true identity. Whoever did this to Claire must have been living on the ranch at the time. Well, the police are sure of it; what tracks they found at the site of Claire's murder led only to and from the ranch." He reached out and took my hand between his own. "Honey, if you are afraid or would rather not do this thing, then say so. I don't want there to be any pressure on you. I certainly have no wish to lose another daughter."

No pressure... huh... my unknown twin is murdered, and the father I met for the first time just yesterday asks me this crazy and totally ridiculous favour—the most astonishing favour. To impersonate my dead twin sister in an attempt to catch her killer and no pressure he says!

I picked up my teaspoon and twiddled with it, turning and twisting it. My father reached out and covered my agitated hand with his own. "Nicola… Nicky... honey?" he queried, softly, "are you okay, kiddo?" I shook my head not daring to speak as tears threatened to choke me, it was all too much. Oblivious to the stares of other people around us, he placed his arm around my shoulders comfortingly. I turned my face into his shoulder and breathed in his scent. It was amazing that this man, a complete stranger to me, yet so, so familiar, smelt... right. His scent told me he was my father, my very own flesh and blood. Sighing, I shivered slightly. Up until yesterday, I had had a flesh and blood twin, my own sister… now dead. How could I *not* do what he asked of me?

Gathering my thoughts, I leant back in my chair. "The photo on the news, not cool, everyone knows what happened."

"No, honey, they don't. All that was released was a press statement saying that Claire had suffered a serious life threatening injury after a riding accident."

"Why? I mean why not let the police interview everyone and well, do the things they usually do in a case like this?"

"I have spoken to the top guy... we go way back you know? College and so forth. He has no clues, no motive and no forensic evidence. I am convinced this is our best bet for flushing out the killer."

"It's rather unusual, I am certain the police over here in England would never agree to such a plan."

"Well now, as to that, I don't reckon they think you'll say yes to my plan, honey, but hey, I want you to make up your own mind. I'll go along with whatever you decide. If you returned with me to the States, well, we can still take the time to get to know one another."

I nodded absently. I was still musing about how I would impersonate my twin.

"What about my accent? Claire was American born and bred," I said, pointing out what I considered a major flaw in his plan.

He placed his palm against my face and caressed my cheek with his thumb. "Thank you, Nicola. If you had said no, I would still want you to come back with me. Honey, I'm so glad that you will return with me to see your family home and help catch your twin's killer. It would have been just terrible leaving you behind especially after we had met for the very first time!"

What? "I haven't actually agreed to this as yet, Father. You shouldn't jump to conclusions. You know that you could have flown over to meet me any time previous to Claire's death." I then added sadly, "I might have had a chance to get to know my twin if you'd done that."

"Sure, honey, I know but Susan… she..." His voice trailed off as he shrugged. "Feeble huh, a man like me afraid of an itsy-bitsy female!" he said, half smiling.

I didn't return his smile. "The accent," I reminded him, a trifle tartly.

"Well now, I guess you could just whisper maybe... you know, pretend your voice was affected by the attack? Look, honey, there will be detectives and doctors to advise us back home, let's not get hung up on incidentals. Besides, your voice is the same as Claire's, it's only your accent that's different."

Then it occurred to me, this was how my father had separated his twin daughters. So we had simply been *incidentals* to him, my sister and I, and thus our fates were sealed.

THE NEXT COUPLE of days were difficult for me. Emotionally I was a wreck. My life was in turmoil. I took a leave of absence so that at least the pressure of work was not an issue. I was lucky; I owned my apartment outright and my mother would fall over herself to help me financially, especially now that she was so full of guilt.

My father told me as much as he could about Claire. Her likes and dislikes, her taste in clothes, music, books, and even men. She had a sort of fiancée for goodness sake. When I pointed out the difficulties this could pose should I impersonate Claire, my father pointed out that Matt had found Claire dead, he would be in on our secret.

Why is it, I thought crossly, that men never seem to see the emotional bigger picture? Has it not occurred to my father that Matt might have a problem with me? I am the mirror image of the woman he loved. The poor man will have to pretend to the world that I am Claire and that he is not suffering, torn apart by her death. He had taken off after the police had questioned him, but had returned in time to agree to my father's hair-brained scheme. Why was I agreeing to it? I suppose that I was desperate to please him, I wanted my father to love *me.*

My mother left me numerous messages, posted through my door at regular intervals by the ever loyal Jenkins. I really could not deal with the feelings of anger and betrayal she aroused in me just at the moment. So I was particularly distressed to see her car, complete with Jenkins, parked outside my apartment on my return later that day.

My mother had her own key to my flat but, up until today, she had only used it for entry into the apartment with my permission. Outside the front door, I paused and took a deep breath before entering.

She was sitting at an angle on the couch, knees together, back ramrod straight, facing me as I walked in through the door. She half rose and then sat back down on the couch. With some surprise, I realised that she was nervous. "Forgive me for intruding like this, Nicola dear, but we must talk."

I threw my jacket onto a chair and kicked off my black sling backs. "Okay, so talk."

"Please don't be like this, Nicola," she pleaded.

"Look, Mother, I am really tired. You have lied to me for years and because of those lies, you have denied me the right to know my own twin-sister and I don't think I can ever forgive you for that."

She raised a well-manicured hand to her head and massaged her temple. "Nicky, you forget that I have lost a daughter."

"I have lost the opportunity to ever know my twin..." I interrupted angrily, "....and *you* gave up any rights when you abandoned her as a baby!"

She nodded sadly, "I totally agree. You cannot say anything to me that I haven't already said to myself. I have spent the last twenty years questioning my decision. However, the fact remains that I was given no choice in the matter, it was a case of one baby or none at all."

"I can't believe that my father would be that cruel." But, even as I said the words, I knew that I doubted them.

"I did not come here to bicker with you. I am leaving now, Nicola, and I just want to say this to you, without interruption if you please. I know more than anyone what a charismatic and charming man your father can be and more than anyone, I know how ruthless he is. Be aware of that, Nicola, and promise me that you will think very carefully before you do anything that he asks of you. Remember that I love you, despite what you think of me. If you need me, you only have to call."

She stood up, gathered her coat and bag and started moving towards the door. She stopped briefly and offered me her cheek to kiss, which I dutifully did and then she was gone, a waft of Chanel No 5 lingering in the air. I stood still for a while chewing a nail. I guess I needed someone to blame, and so I blamed my mother.

I think it was at that moment that I fully made up my mind to go along with my father's crazy plan. I would impersonate my twin in an attempt to catch her killer.

Did I do this to spite my mother? Perhaps. I don't really know but, although it might have been *partly* that, I like to think my decision was solely for my twin sister, Claire.

3

Grief

After the tiring but luxurious First Class flight to New York on a Pan-Am 707, my father ushered me into a taxi which took us to the Waldorf Astoria Hotel. This is where we were to stay overnight before taking the Keedon executive Lear Jet to Phoenix, Arizona.

The hotel was simply amazing and although my mother always liked to stay in luxury accommodations when she travelled, I can honestly say that I had never stayed anywhere quite so splendid when travelling with her. The Waldorf was magnificent and nothing was too much trouble for the staff. Despite the comfort level, I did not sleep well that night. It may have been the dry air due to the air conditioning system, a feature that I was unused to back home, or it may have been the excited stress at my present unusual situation. Consequently, I was exhausted by the time we left for the airport the following day.

The flight was an ideal time for my father to fill me in on 'who was who' at the ranch, or 'The Plomosa' as it was named. Due to my lack of sleep, I seriously wondered how much that my father told me about Claire, the ranch and the people who lived there, would sink in and stick in my travel weary brain.

There was Sarah the housekeeper, who had married my father's cousin, my second cousin, I guess, who had been a pilot during the war. After the war had ended in 1945, Mr. and Mrs. Williams had set up home together in Scottsdale, Arizona. After her husband had died of cancer only a few years later, the feisty Scottish woman had come to stay and basically never left, taking the role of housekeeper and becoming a valued member of the family. There was Kate, who also lived in; my father described her as more of a general assistant. Matthew Lane I already knew of. He ran the cattle side of the ranch and although he bunked at the ranch, he was living in Flagstaff since Claire had died. My father told me that he thought that keeping the secret of Claire's murder was a difficult task for Matt. There was also a Liam O'Donnell and he was in charge of the tourist side of things. Apparently The Plomosa was a new kind of tourist concept—a 'Dude Ranch' which meant people could stay in bunkhouses—luxury models— and get the whole cowboy ranch experience.

I was concerned about Sarah, the housekeeper, and Kate, the general assistant; they knew Claire well and I would have to be very wary around them. My father also went over Claire's likes and dislikes with regards to music, books, food etc. Her music preferences showed me that she was definitely not a *cool cat.* Claire liked country and western. Not a big surprise there seeing that she had grown up on a ranch in Arizona. Claire liked Elvis too but, then, who didn't! Books now that did surprise me, for her favourite was mine as well, *Sense and Sensibility* by Jane Austen. Her food tastes were similar to my own except for the fact my sister had become a dedicated vegetarian. Rather a surprising thing on a cattle ranch I thought. My father drew a picture of a pliable and dreamy girl. I was rather disappointed because she sounded too much like a 'wishy-washy' girl to me. On the other hand, I mused this was a 'Daddy's view' of Claire. She must have had some strength of will to become a vegetarian amongst all those meat eating rednecks, especially since she was living amidst them on a cattle ranch.

We were met at the Phoenix airport by two plain clothes detectives. They whisked us through the back of the airport to a waiting car that had blacked-out windows. Everything up until now had had a fictional feel, but as I climbed into the unmarked car, I realised the enormity of what I was undertaking. Could I go through with this? I was tired from the flight and from all the overwhelming emotion of the last few days. It suddenly dawned on me that I could not possibly carry on with this stupid plan. How could I possibly impersonate Claire? I would need to be insane to do this.

We were to be driven first to the police precinct and then on to the hospital where Claire had been taken after she had been found.

Travelling into the city, I was surprised by the amazingly wide roads and the speed of the American drivers. The cars and their passengers travelled past in a steady flow, unlike at home in England where a car was still a luxury item that only a minority of people could afford.

After a drive into and through the city, we finally turned onto a ramp on the side of a large red brick building and drove down a concrete slope into an underground garage. The older detective jumped from the car and whisked open my door helping me out and hurrying me into an open lift. My father and the other detective followed on behind. The lift glided upwards and we travelled in silence until we stopped at the seventh floor, emerging into a quiet corridor. A woman wearing a plain black suit met us and we were ushered rapidly along to a room and asked to wait. Presently, a tall slim man entered and after shaking my father's hand, he asked us both to sit. The thin man introduced himself to me as Chief Stewart and, fixing his astute gaze on me, he studied me a while. He continued to stare for some time, still not speaking and I began to fidget, feeling uncomfortable. Finally he spoke, "The likeness is extraordinary Miss Keedon, do..."

I interrupted him, "St. Clare."

"I apologise, Miss St. Clare, of course."

"Nicola, you're a Keedon," my father said irritably.

The Chief and I both ignored him. "Are you quite sure you wish to go through with this double act, Miss St. Clare?" he asked me quietly.

"Do you think it will work?" I asked.

"Well now, ma'am, up until the moment I met you just now, I was totally against this whole idea of your father's. Now... well, it will be dangerous... you do understand that, Miss St. Clare, extremely dangerous. The person who killed your sister will surely try again, once he or she, finds they have not succeeded. I shall, of course, place a detective with you at all times. She will pretend to be your physiotherapist. I must tell you straight though, Miss St. Clare, that I would be much happier if we just announced that your sister had been murdered and a full murder inquiry opened."

My father started to say something like, "See here, Stewart!" but I interrupted him.

"Have you collected any evidence at all, Mr. Stewart?"

The Chief looked at me with interest, "None I am sorry to say, Miss St. Clare. Your sister was wearing gloves so there were no traces under her nails. We think that her murderer also wore gloves."

"My father said that you were certain the killer came from the ranch. Why is that?" I asked.

"Where we found Claire there were no tracks leading off in any other direction except your sister's from The Plomosa. Your sister was found in a small canyon on the outer edge of the ranch, on Pinto Rock. The trail leading there is one used frequently by Plomosa hands and occasionally tourists. There were no truck or horse tracks leading from the ranch to Iron

Canyon and, before you ask, Miss St. Clare, there were no tourists staying there at the time of your sister's death. The household were at breakfast together around the time of the murder."

"Mmm, yes I see, so you have no suspects?"

"Well, O'Donnell has no alibi but your father vouches for him." I looked up at my father and he nodded his head. However, I tucked that little nugget of information away for later discussion with him.

Right now I had more important things to think about. "Chief, I wish to view my sister's body today." I heard my father's sharp intake of breath and turned to him. "I must, I *have* to see her," I told him. He looked at the Chief and, after a moment, he gave a brief nod.

The Chief cleared his throat, "Very well, Miss St. Clare, if you're absolutely sure about this?" I nodded. "Okay then, I will telephone ahead to the Flagstaff Medical Centre and arrange that for you now."

"Thank you." I stood up and stretched out my hand which he shook firmly before he moved to the door, holding it open for our exit.

After a short while, we were on our way once again, this time to the hospital where Claire's body was being kept under guard.

From there, I was to take her place and deceive her killer into thinking that he, or she, had failed with the attempt on Claire's life, by tempting him, or her, to try again—*was I quite mad?*

I would become Claire and by impersonating her, perhaps I would finally get to know my twin sister; this was the only thing left that I could do for her.

I had imagined a journey of half an hour or so from the police headquarters to the hospital. After an hour of driving, I asked how much longer it would take before we were at our destination.

"Less than an hour now, ma'am. Flagstaff is about one

hundred and forty miles from Phoenix y'know." I did not know—this country was simply vast!

There were two detectives, one was a tall, handsome black guy named Hank. He had a New York accent which I discovered only after my father had asked him which part of New York he hailed from. The other one, the driver, was an older man with a long horse-like face, a grizzled and tough looking individual who looked as if he could take care of anything that came his way. He said very little, spoke quietly and I felt safe with him driving the car. Hank called him 'Mr. Ed.' It was some kind of private joke between the pair of them. I gave myself up to the amazing views beyond the window of the car. Snow lay in patches on the ground despite the fact it was nearly the end of March. We skirted the edge of a pine forest which appeared to go on for miles and in the distance, a large snow-capped mountain stood tall. Not the scenery I had been expecting in Arizona. I had thought to find desert and flat grazing land.

"Does this forest have a name?" I asked my father.

"It sure does, hon'. That there is the Coconino National Forest and those snowy mountains in the distance are the San Francisco Peaks. You'll be able to see Humphreys Peak once we reach Flagstaff. That's the highest mountain at just less than thirteen thousand feet. After we leave the hospital, it's not far to The Plomosa, which is out of Flagstaff on Highway Eighty Nine."

Despite all my fatigue and the ordeal that I knew lay ahead, I was excited. This beautiful country was the land of my birth; it was in my blood and bones and I felt that I had finally come home.

Once again it was down into an underground car park. This time, however, a wheelchair was fetched for me because the police thought it would conceal my identity better than if I was walking. People rarely stared at a person in a wheelchair I was told by Mr. Ed. I was lifted carefully into the chair and they wrapped me in a blanket that covered my head and shadowed my face. I was then wheeled into the lift. We travelled silently up in the *elevator* as I was now remembering to call it, getting into my American persona.

When the doors slid open, the hustle and bustle of hospital life rushed in on me. Swiftly, I was pushed along the corridor, weaving in and out between people. Finally, we turned into a quiet corridor and on through a pair of swinging double doors and into yet another corridor. This part of the hospital was very quiet as it was not open to the public. The smell of disinfectant and some other slightly sweet, sickly scent was much stronger here I noticed. At the end of the corridor, a doctor, the Medical Examiner, in a white hospital coat awaited us. He turned and held open the door so that my wheelchair could enter the room. The blanket was removed from my head, and I saw that we were in a plain and clinical looking room.

In the centre of the room stood a hospital trolley with a shrouded figure laid upon it; my eyes were riveted to the shrouded mound. The Medical Examiner spoke to me but I could not take in what he was saying, though I nodded automatically. He reached for the white cloth and pulled it back. I wanted to stop him, not cool—*I wasn't ready yet!*

Suddenly there she was, my twin sister Claire. She lay there as if she was simply sleeping. I stretched out a finger and gently laid the back of it against her cheek, her pale skin was cold and unyielding. I was jolted. Not sleeping, of course, but dead—my face and my hair, dead. I swayed. I felt a hand slip under my elbow and shook it free. Leaning forward, I gazed at her hungrily, wanting the knowledge of her physical form… of her reality. I traced my finger over her bow shaped eyebrows, *mine.* I stroked the plains of her cheeks, *mine.* I touched her pale, pale lips, *mine.* I bent to kiss them, so, so cold. Suddenly her voice seemed to fill my head and I heard her words, "*sister… at last my sister, ah, too late, too late!*"

"NICKY... Nicky, sweetheart. I should never have allowed her to do this!"

"Okay, Mr. Keedon, it's just a simple faint—there and she's back with us. Nicola, how do you feel? Drink this, it is only water, yes that's right, sip it slowly—how do you feel—better?"

I sat up and stared around me. "Did you hear?" I whispered, dazed.

"Hear what, hon'?" My father asked with a frown.

"Claire, *she spoke to me*!"

"Aw now... hon... come on!"

"Mr. Keedon, this is quite normal." The doctor hunkered down beside me. "Nicola, lots of people experience hallucinations on the death of a loved one and people often think they see their dead relatives moving and even speaking to them. Is that what happened to you just now?"

I nodded, "Yes, but I didn't imagine it, Claire spoke... s*he spoke to me.*" I appealed to my father holding out my hand to him.

He clasped it in his and raised it to his lips before saying, "No, hon', no, Claire didn't move or speak or anything. Claire is dead, Nicky. Honey, look... I want to take you back to England. The strain of this is all too much for you, it was a crazy, crazy plan. I can see that now."

"No! No! No! I am fine. You believe what you like, but I am going to find my sister's murderer, just as she wants me to!" I glared at him while the doctor patted my shoulder and shook his head at my father as he made to speak to me again. Finally he cleared his throat, nodded and turned away. I glanced back at the shrouded form of my twin and made my silent oath to her and to this day, I swear that she heard me. The doctor assured me of his discretion regarding my identity, shaking my hand before ushering us out into the hospital corridor. Once again I was covered by the blanket and wheeled into the bowels of the hospital. The next stop would be the room where I would change, becoming my twin Claire.

THE ROUTE back to the main part of the hospital was travelled in uneasy silence. I could sense my father's worry. After numerous twists and turns, we came to a room and I was manoeuvred inside. A young man sat beside an empty bed, next to it stood a bedside cupboard on which stood a vase of beautiful hothouse lilies. A night-dress was laid out on the pillow. The young man stood up, his burning gaze riveted on me. He held his hat in his hands, which he turned and twisted agitatedly. "Jeepers creepers," he gasped, turning white as he stared fixedly at me.

"Matt, hi there, son, how're you doing?" My father went over to him and clasped the young man's shoulder.

"Um, I'm okay I guess, Mr. Keedon. Jeez, man... it is Claire!"

I held out my hand shakily. I didn't like this young man's reaction at all. "You must be Matthew Lane. I'm Nicola and I am so sorry for your loss," I said as gently as I could.

He stumbled forward and I noticed that his hand shook as he took mine. "N-Nicola, right? Shit, but you are the spitting image of Claire. I'm real sorry, it's just… the shock I guess."

"That's cool, I understand." I patted his hand and let him go. He was a very pleasant looking man, in his late twenties I guessed—fair hair, hazel eyes, even features, he looked a nice type. "I have a couple of questions for you, Matt… is that okay with you?"

He nodded. "Sure."

"Why didn't you tell anyone else at the ranch that Claire was dead after you found her body?" This was something my father had not explained and I had been curious about it ever since he had conceived this plan.

Matt looked at my father who gave him a brief nod. "I was

worried that Claire was dumping me when she didn't arrive for breakfast, so I rode out and followed her horse tracks to Pinto Rock…" Matt stopped speaking. He was obviously distressed; he rubbed his hand over his face before continuing. "I-I... er... found Claire on the flat rock which is about four feet off the ground and about fifty feet in diameter. Sasha was real agitated down on soft ground pawing at the edge as if she wanted to climb up there y'know?" I nodded, I hated to upset the guy, but I needed to understand this. "I felt for Claire's pulse but I knew she was dead when I looked at her, her throat... so I grabbed Sasha's reins and started back to the ranch to get help. That's when I met Mr. Keedon and told him what I had found." Matt finished talking and pulled a handkerchief from his jeans pocket giving his nose a loud blow.

My father continued the tale. "Matt lead me to Claire and I began to think about you, Nicky, and how it might be possible to trick her killer into thinking Claire was still alive. I persuaded Matt to keep quiet about the murder until after I had spoken to Chief Stewart."

Matt looked at me and said, "I didn't want to go along with this charade you know. I've been bunking down in town rather than spending time up at The Plomosa since it happened. Just so's you know, I thought this whole plan was crazy hogwash but, now that I see the likeness, well y'know, it jus' might work at that!"

I put my hand on his arm and gave him a squeeze before turning to the two detectives. "So, what now?" I asked.

Mr. Ed. answered me, "You are to change into night clothes and get into bed and await Detective Jules Danker who will be along real soon. She's going home with you tomorrow as your physiotherapist. We will stand guard outside your room tonight. A statement will be made to the press to the effect that you remember nothing at all of the fall from your horse or of anyone attacking you. You will dismiss the whole idea as ridiculous to anyone at the ranch and appear not to take the suggestion by the doctors that there are signs of strangulation around your throat seriously."

"What about the evidence? My throat for instance, the plan is that I whisper, yeah, due to my injury and to cover my English accent."

Hank conferred with his colleague. "You could say your scarf must have got caught when you fell and, while you were unconscious, your horse dragged you."

Matt interrupted. "That's plumb crazy. Sasha would never have dragged Claire and everyone will know that, her horse adored her!"

Hank sighed. "I suggest that if asked, you could say that a snake spooked the horse which most people would understand. Now we're gonna wait outside, Nicky, and allow you to become Claire. You can still change your mind you know… last chance."

I felt my father's eyes on me. I took a moment to reflect before I spoke. "No… I'm cool, I'll do this. You wait outside and I will be ready in a jiffy." As they all turned to leave the room, I overheard Matt whisper to my father. "What's a 'Jiffy'?"

Hey, my first lesson in Anglo American language difference. I must be so careful while playing the role of my American sister; American *was* another language.

4

Nervous

I did not sleep well that night. The bandage they put around my neck was uncomfortable and I was so nervous about the following day. I still had not met the detective, Jules Danker, as her flight from Vegas had been delayed. Apparently, she specialised in undercover work and was unknown in this area. As far as I knew, it was unheard of to have police women like her in England and I was intrigued to meet with her.

I watched some TV before I settled down for the night. A news announcement was made that Claire Keedon was out of danger and was likely to be released from the hospital the following day. There was a brief summary of the accident and an old news shot of my father leaving the ranch in a car while waving at the camera. The media would hopefully lose interest now. As far as they were concerned, Claire being alive was no news... if only it were true.

The police had stated that they were prepared to go along with the charade for about a month. If the killer had made no move by then, they would move in and begin to question everyone at the ranch. One month. I wondered what would be the end result of this charade. Unfortunately, I possess a vivid imagination.

JULES DANKER LOOKED as though she would be more at home teaching sports in a girl's school than working as an undercover detective. She had an open and honest sincerity about her. She was very reassuring but, at the same time, she made the danger seem very real and my apprehension grew. We waited for my father to arrive and when he did, I dressed in the clothes he brought—Claire's clothes. I was wheeled down through the main entrance, this time without the blanket over me. A long black car awaited us, complete with a driver. There were two photographers waiting and although they took pictures, nobody expected me to speak. My father made a brief statement to them after which I was safely stowed in the back of the car with Jules.

Even after turning off the main road and onto the private drive that I assumed led to the ranch house, it took another ten minutes for me to get my first view of The Plomosa. We swept around a bend in the road and there it was; I was captivated! A long low building constructed of soft golden stone and finished with white weatherboard cladding sat solidly and comfortably in the gentle dip of land. A veranda with a green roof ran around three sides of the building. It was a pretty and no doubt, functional house and I loved it at first sight. The car carried on around to the back of the ranch house and parked in front of a block of barn type garages. I hung back as we all made our way towards the house. My father turned to look for me and slid an arm around my shoulders giving me a squeeze. "Don't forget to call me Daddy and stop saying 'cool'. It's not a term Claire used," he whispered.

I looked at him aghast; this was the first time he'd mentioned Claire's name for him. Why hadn't I thought to ask about such a fundamental thing as, 'what did my sister call you'? It made me wonder what other things had I neglected to find out about. Well, it was much too late to worry now.

Two collie dogs ran to greet us and seemed very interested in my scent, sniffing about my feet and whining with their tails held down. My father patted them both and pushed past them guiding me to the back door.

We entered the house via the kitchen. A pretty girl, I guessed her to be about my own age, just into her twenties perhaps, was standing at the sink peeling potatoes. She looked up and grinned when we came in. This must be Kate, I thought. She dropped what she was doing and came straight over to give me a hug. "Carl said you've no recollection at all of what happened out there, you poor thing!"

My attention was distracted away from her by a woman's sharp yell. A small plump, middle-aged lady shot towards me and pushing Kate aside, enveloped me in her arms, weeping as she patted my back. "Och you gave us such a scare, Claire lass, you naughty wee girl… so are you all right, my dear? I've changed the bedding but otherwise I've left your room just as it was. Yon nurse can have the blue guest room next to your room. Why don't you go up now and have a nice rest; I'll bring you a wee drop o' tea in a while. What d'you say, Claire?"

Not a lot it seemed, for just as I opened my mouth to reply, she was off again. "You've a bandage then. Is it very sore, your poor wee throat? Aye, well, I suppose you would be…"

"Sarah will you stop your blasted blethering woman and let me into my own home!" Father had had enough it seemed, although I noticed he spoke with a grin on his face. It was all I could do to stop myself from falling into hysterical laughter, nerves on my part no doubt. It seemed though that the grin was what was expected and Sarah laughed and waved us through the kitchen.

"Go on then the lot of you, away and I'll bring you through your coffee and Claire's tea.

I was relieved I was expected to drink tea and not the bitter brew my father called coffee. As I moved into the interior of the house, I found that beyond the kitchen, the floors were all of honeyed wood, solid and warm. A wide staircase rose upwards from the left and closed double doors were on the right of them. In front, were more double doors which stood flung wide, leading into a sunny sitting room that was spacious and light; woven rugs in mellow coloured tones were on the floor and a fire burned in the huge stone hearth. Large comfortable looking leather covered arm chairs were placed on either side of the fireplace with a huge Chesterfield sofa facing the hearth. I went into this welcoming room and sat at one end of the Chesterfield. Curling up, I kicked off my shoes and drew my feet up under myself. The gesture was truly my own but my father said, "Ah, it's good to see you curled up in your favourite spot again, Claire." I noticed his eyes looking rather moist as he turned away from me.

Jules Danker sat down next to me and winked as she spoke. "After your tea, I want to begin your treatment, Claire." I nodded and smiled at her.

JULES CLOSED the double sitting room doors and checked the windows were all closed before coming to sit next to me once again. We were alone; everyone had dispersed about their own work and left us to ourselves. "Now then, Claire... and I shall call you Claire the whole while, this is so that I don't slip up on your name."

"I understand," I said, quietly.

"Good. Now, I want to know wherever and whenever you go anywhere, even when you go to the bathroom, is that understood, Claire?"

"Yes, but won't it look odd—you following me everywhere?"

"No, as far as everyone is concerned, I am here to nurse you and they will expect me to fuss over you. I want you to make it clear to one and all that you have no memory of the attack. Call it an accident if people ask about it; the killer won't be so desperate if he thinks you don't remember him—or her."

"Cool, but how will the killer make a move with you there protecting me all the time?"

"I will appear to take breaks. No one will suspect a thing. Don't worry, Claire, that's my job."

"God, this is all so weird!"

"I'm sure—look just try to relax—you're doing really well! Do you feel ready to look around upstairs yet, you know, get to know the layout of the place? We can say you're showing me around if we meet anyone while we poke about."

We left the sitting room and explored, firstly all the downstairs rooms and then the upstairs.

Finally, I opened a bedroom door onto what I knew had to have been Claire's bedroom. Jules put her hand on my arm. "I'll leave you alone for a bit. If you need me, I'll be next door in the blue guest suite." She said this in a good imitation of Sarah's Scottish accent and I giggled.

Claire's room, her private place, was painted a soft primrose yellow and the woodwork was a brilliant white. The curtains were white with bright yellow daisies scattered randomly; they were moving gently in the cool breeze from the partly raised sash window. The bed was covered in a white cotton throw, with central embroidery which included a circle of yellow daisies. A solid pale wooden desk sat under the window. I picked up a paperweight and looked at its intricate inner world of swirling gold and yellow. My fingers trailed over pens and flicked open note pads. I pulled open drawers with increasing urgency, looking—but looking for what?

I stopped looking the third drawer down; I had found what I

sought, Claire's diary. I hesitated and then closed the drawer again. Not yet. It was too soon. I turned around and leant back against the desk; my gaze taking in the room and its contents. My sister's room—this was the closest that I would ever get to her now, the only link left with her in this life—except, my thoughts strayed to the diary, later!

Purposefully, I moved across to the closet and opened the door; a light popped on inside. On the top shelf sat a motley collection of teddies and dolls, they stared mournfully back at me. Next to them sat a pretty pink jewellery box. Lifting the lid, tinkling music began to play. Gently, I closed the lid. I cast my eyes over the hanging rail and thumbed through the selection of clothes. A faint almond smell wafted out. I closed my eyes and breathed in her scent, my sister's smell. So familiar, so comforting and yet, I had never known her. Do people retain scent memories as babes I wondered, was it possible that I retained some memory of her smell from babyhood, perhaps even from the womb? I closed the closet and opened the adjacent door. A pink bathroom and a walk-in shower, wow what luxury! A pale pink towelling robe hung on the back of the door, Claire's. I fingered it sadly for a moment and then turned to the cupboard over the pink basin.

Jars of face creams and shampoos, conditioners, tweezers, etc. stood neatly in a line upon the shelf. I picked up a jar of face cream, took off the lid and smelled it. I did the same with all of the bottles and jars. A very pale pink lipstick seemed to beckon me to try it on. It was okay but made me look so much younger than my twenty odd years. Not how I wanted to look but then, of course, I must try and look as Claire did. The picture I was building in my head of Claire was someone fresh, natural and slightly more immature in her tastes compared to my own. I turned back to the mirror and applied another light coat of the pale pearly lipstick.

I had noticed a photograph beside Claire's bed, so I closed

the bathroom door and went to the bed reaching for the picture as I sat down. I stared at my likeness. It was as if someone had taken a photograph of me and from then onwards, the memory of the moment had vanished. The picture was of a much younger Claire, sitting upon a horse. Our father stood beside her holding the halter at the bit. He was grinning up at her, his face alight with laughter and love but also something else—pride. Claire, her face, my face, turned towards the camera, head thrown back, blue eyes shining, full of merriment. The honeyed tones of her sable brown hair glinted gold in the sun, her hair was tossed casually over one shoulder and tucked behind her ear. How could I ever know her now? My twin was gone forever; I realised my face was awash with tears and I lay down, giving way to my grief.

I HAD GONE to bed straight after a quiet supper, eating with just my father and Jules. I fell asleep quickly and slept deeply until I awoke during the wee small hours. There was moonlight streaming through the window and onto my face. I stumbled out of bed and closed the curtains. With a jolt, I remembered that I had closed them before climbing into bed the evening before. Someone must have been in my room and opened them again. Just as I pulled the curtains together, a movement down in the darkness below caught my eye. Opening the curtains a little, I saw a dark shape detach itself from the shadows and turn to stare up at me. Whoever it was, their face was clouded by shadow. Disturbed, I quickly pulled the curtains closed and ran to the door. I opened it a crack and peered out onto the landing, listening. I could hear the faint hum of machinery, a refrigerator perhaps somewhere in the bowels of the house. Quietly closing the door again, I realised there was no key in the lock; I determined to find the key in the morning. Uneasy, I lay in my bed, wakeful and wondering whether I should wake Jules or not. Perhaps the person outside had, in fact, been Jules. Who had been in my room while I slept and opened my curtains? You are being silly I told myself, it was probably Sarah. Perhaps Claire always slept with the curtains open and she had opened them to be kind. With that reassuring thought, I turned over and finally slept.

When I woke, it was to bright sunlight shining in through the window—my curtains were open once again. I fetched Claire's pink robe and went next door to Jules's room. I tapped lightly on the door and was reassured to hear her voice calling me in.

"Claire, did you sleep well?"

I shook my head. "No, actually something strange happened during the night."

Jules's look sharpened as she sat up in her bed and patted it invitingly. I closed the door and went and joined her. "So tell me," she said.

"When I went to bed last night, I closed the curtains, but in the middle of the night, I woke up and found that they were open." I glanced at Jules, wondering if she thought I was being daft. She nodded encouragingly, so I continued. "When I got up to close them, I looked outside and I saw someone. I think they were watching my window."

"Could you tell whether it was a man or a woman?"

"No, it was too dark and whoever it was stood in the shadows. I was hoping you'd say it was you watching out for me."

She shook her head. "Sorry to disappoint you, kiddo, but it wasn't me. Anything else?"

"Yes, when I woke up this morning, my curtains were open again."

"How'd you mean, 'again'?"

"Well I thought that Sarah had opened them."

"It's unlikely she would come into your room in the middle of the night," Jules frowned as she spoke.

I nodded my agreement. "Exactly my thoughts. In fact, I convinced myself she had opened them last night and that the person outside was you simply keeping an eye out."

"Say what?"

"Sorry, it's an English expression, meaning that you are looking out for me."

"Hmm, watch those English expressions, especially 'cool'; you could give the whole game away. If anything else happens out of the norm, come straight to me. Don't wait 'til morning next time. Hold on, I've got something for you that I forgot to give you last night." Jules jumped out of bed and pulled her suitcase out from underneath it. She opened it up and took out a black walkie-talkie set. "Here, this is my latest spy gadget, take it, it's for you." She held out a hand set. "Now if anything odd, however small or insignificant, happens to you, just press the talk button and alert me; I'll be with you in seconds."

I took the hand piece from her. "Thanks, I feel safer now that I have this with me. Should I ask Sarah about the curtains?"

Jules cocked her head and thought for a moment before answering me. "Yeah, I think so but wait until there's no one else about listening in. Right, you'd better go get dressed. I'll knock for you in say, twenty minutes?"

"Yup, that will be fine. I'll just take a quick shower."

Jules called me back just as I was about to leave the room. "Claire, you've removed the bandage from your throat. Put it back on and don't let anyone else see you without it, it's way too soon to remove it." My hand flew to my throat. I had indeed removed the wretched thing to enable me to sleep more comfortably. I wondered if the person in my room last night had noticed it was gone.

It seemed everyone at The Plomosa kept early morning hours. Jules and I were the last two down for breakfast. We ate in the kitchen and despite our polite protests, we were waited on by Kate. She was a chatty girl and we learned that my father had gone off early on business and that he wouldn't be back until late morning. I was a little hurt by this information. Why hadn't he awoken me to say goodbye... why had he gone at all on my first day at the ranch? We also learned that Sarah had driven into Flagstaff to fetch the weekly groceries. I remembered to whisper and asked Kate if she knew where the key to my room was. She was surprised to learn it was not in the lock on the door.

I wanted to go back upstairs and start investigating Claire's diary, but Jules was worried about the unlocked bedroom doors. Her own room key was also missing. She suggested that she drive us into Flagstaff and buy some more locks thereby ensuring that only she and I would have keys to my door. I was quite excited at the idea of looking around the American town, so I went upstairs to grab a jacket and my purse.

We drove around to the front of the house in Claire's car, a sleek red Cadillac. I itched to drive but Jules thought it best that she drove until I was familiar with the road lay out. We passed a cowboy complete with a western style hat, walking towards the stables off to the right. He was a tall man, broad shouldered and masculine, although I couldn't see more because his features were hidden under the shadow of his large hat. He stopped and stared as we passed him. As I turned back to watch him, Jules said, "Wow, he looks kinda cute, let's hope he's not the one."

"The one?"

"Yeah, you know, our murderer."

"Oh," I said. Somehow the trip was spoiled by that comment and we didn't speak again until we entered Flagstaff.

Flagstaff is a tourist town where real people live. At least that's how my father described it to me while travelling over on the plane from England.

We pulled into a large car park outside the mall. Inside were a variety of shops including a JC Penney store and it was with great excitement that I walked inside. JCP was world famous as the archetypal American store. Claire's jeans were a little tight on me around the bum, so I decided to buy a couple of pairs of jeans that were a more comfortable fit. I also bought some cute checked shirts to wear while I was on the ranch. Luckily Claire and I shared the same shoe size, so I could make good use of her shoes. We also had the same 'C' cup bust measurement. I had only packed a few pairs of slacks, some sneakers and underwear for the trip over, since I knew that I would be using Claire's wardrobe once here.

I made my selection of clothing and headed for the changing room. Jules had gone off to locate locks for our bedrooms. As I came out of the changing area carrying my choices, I passed a young woman who spun around catching hold of my arm, a delighted grin on her face.

"Claire, well, hi there! I thought it was you. Howdy, I haven't seen you in ages! You still dating Matt? Joe and I split up. Are you guy's gonna be holding' your Pa's birthday party this year?"

"Hi," I whispered back, terrified.

"Oh my God, Claire, I forgot you were in some kinda accident weren't you—you okay now, hon'—what actually happened?"

"I'd rather not talk right now, sorry, my throat y' know?" I whispered back, trying to copy her drawl.

She looked stricken. "Hey, I'm real sorry, Claire, does it hurt you bad? Stupid, Leanne, of course it does! Look, you just take care of yourself all right? I'll ring you in a couple of days. I wanna talk to you about 'the dish.' Now then, don't you look dumb, you know *who* I mean. I thought, well, I'm fancy-free; I might as well have a crack at him. After all, I go out and help out with the 'teens' don't I?" She winked lasciviously. "Know what I mean?"

I nodded knowingly and grimaced touching my throat. "Talk soon, Leanne, bye for now," I whispered with my drawl and then I spun around and walked rapidly towards the till. What on earth did she mean by the 'teens'? I had to get out of there quickly before I met anyone else who knew Claire.

Jules was coming across the floor and waved. I whispered frantically, telling her what had happened.

"Hey, you handled the situation well. I can't see what the fuss is about, just calm down!" She patted my arm reassuringly and after paying for our purchases, we made our way back to the car. Jules had both locks and bolts in her bag. She promised to fit them as soon as we got back and I volunteered to help. Travelling homewards, I tried to find out more about Jules. She gave little away as to her background and was evasive when I questioned her about her past life and family connections. I assumed this was due to the sensitive nature of her job but it made bonding with her frustrating. Although I liked her, our roles due to the situation, made any friendship between us strained.

Sarah was back when we arrived at The Plomosa, busily unpacking groceries. "Och, there ye are then, Claire love, what'll you want for yer lunch the day?"

I shrugged. "Just a sandwich please, Sarah," I whispered.

"All righty and the same for you then, Miss?" she asked Jules who nodded her reply.

"Sarah," I asked in my perpetual whisper, "did you open the curtains in my room last night?"

"Open yer curtains? No lass… why would I do such a thing… why d'you ask?" She turned her beady eye on me.

"Well, somebody did last night," I said.

"Och, lass, why did ye not lock yer door?"

"There is no key in either Miss Keedon's door or my own. I think Claire mentioned that to Kate this morning," Jules answered.

"Well, 'tis most strange, most strange indeed because the keys were there the day before yesterday when I cleaned upstairs. I am certain sure they were." Sarah wagged her head to emphasise the point.

"We must tell Mr. Carl when he gets back; he will be worried."

"I have bought locks and keys and intend fitting them today, Sarah, so please don't fret," Jules reassured her.

"There are plenty of strong men around here who could have done that for you, lass, you didn't need to go gallivanting off to buy locks and keys! I wish we knew what was happening around here I really do, such carryings on... soon we won't be safe in our beds and that's a fact...." Jules and I crept out of the kitchen and left Sarah to her gloomy mutterings.

5

Ambivalent

While Jules hunted for tools she would need to fit the locks, I decided to take a look at the tourist bunkhouses on the dude section of the ranch. My father had drawn me a map of the ranch layout and I tucked that into the pocket of my new, comfortable jeans and set off, creeping out of the front door so as not to be caught by Sarah and put under house arrest. I needed to walk. I had my walkie-talkie and Jules knew where I was headed. She warned me to be vigilant and I agreed to all her stipulations with regards to time and distance and at last, I was free. There was no doubt life was going to be claustrophobic living under threat as I was.

I walked past the stables and on down a wide track between empty corrals. Though it was a sunny day, it was extremely chilly. The area was beautiful, populated with cedar trees and a backdrop of snow-capped mountains. I felt the tension of the night's drama draining away as I began to enjoy myself. The air was fresh and crisp, sharp with the tang of pine.

I walked for about half a mile or so before I came to a fork in the track. I needed to consult my map. I wanted the left fork in the road and turned in that direction. The bunkhouses and the cookhouse soon came into view. They were long and low, of wooden construction, surrounded by paved and tarmac parking areas. I walked to the nearest building and tried the door. To my disappointment, it was locked. I walked around the side of the building and, shading my eyes, peered inside the window.

"What are you doing?"

I leapt in surprise and turned at the sound of the husky toned voice. It was the same man that Jules and I had passed on the road earlier. Up close, I could see just how attractive he was. Tall and self-assured with short chestnut coloured hair and clear bright cinnamon eyes. He was frowning questioningly. "Shit, you made me jump!" I told him.

"Miss Claire?" He sounded slightly unsure.

Blast, I had forgotten to whisper. I tried again. "Yeah, sorry my voice is a bit… strange since my accident," I said, quietly.

The man looked me over for a long moment before saying, "You'd best be careful 'cause if you go around using bad language like that, you could end up with a sore butt as well as a sore throat."

"I beg your pardon?" I sputtered. Surely I had heard him wrong? He gave a gruff chuckle.

"*English* then is it? Well, Claire, being sassy won't help your case none. You know the rules by now, so jus' watch that mouth, little girl."

I flushed, my skin itching with embarrassment but I nodded meekly. No one had *ever* spoken to me like that before and I had no absolutely no idea how I should respond to him.

The cowboy pushed his hat up with one finger and cocked his head. "Yes, sir?" he suggested.

I went a deeper, ugly shade of red and stared at him dumbly before whispering, "Um 'kay." He tilted his head straight and stood tall—good grief the man must be at least six five! He fastened me with an unblinking stare and I muttered, "Yes, sir," obediently, lowering my eyes away from his intense gaze. I hated myself for being so intimidated by him.

"So how are you feeling after your spin... was real surprised to hear that Sasha threw you. Just what happened out there?"

I remembered Jules's advice to tell everyone I met that I had no recall of the attack. "Um, I'm not feeling so bad now but my throat and neck are still sore. Sasha may have dragged me while I was unconscious? I don't remember *anything* about that morning at all, but how are you today, Mr. O'Donnell?" I hazarded a guess at the man's identity. Once again, I felt myself flush. I felt sure he suspected that I was an imposter. Perhaps this man was Claire's murderer and he was trying to catch me out.

"So formal? Thank you kindly, *Miss Keedon*, I'm jus' fine. Now then, did you want something... were you looking for me?" He gazed steadfastly at me and I squirmed. What was wrong with me? Blast his cool arrogance; just who the hell did he think he was anyway!

"Just checking up on the staff," I quipped cheekily. He raised a lazy eyebrow. What was I doing poking the bear in his den! It wouldn't do to provoke the man but he simply nodded with good humour.

"Okay, missy, d' you want the keys to look the bunkhouses over?"

"Yes," I said with a hiss, somewhat irritated by him now. What was it about this man that made me feel so uncomfortable? O'Donnell took a bunch of keys from his jeans pocket and handed them over to me. I took them and turned to the door fumbling with each key in the lock. He watched me for a while before reaching out a large capable hand, and plucking the keys deftly from me, he sorted out a thin silver key from the rest of the bunch. He proceeded to open the door and stepped back allowing me to enter, handing the bunch of jingling metal back to me without comment.

"Thanks," I mumbled, somewhat ungraciously but he had

already turned and strolled away unhurriedly. I went inside and slammed the door shut, locking it behind me with the key. What an infuriating and unsettling man he was and he threatened to *spank me*, an adult woman!? Could he be Claire's killer? Was that why he made me feel so uneasy?

I leant back against the closed door, shut my eyes and breathed deeply to steady my nerves. I was out here all alone with someone who might be a killer, but then again, he may not be. Surely if he wanted to kill me, he would have come inside and finished me off there and then? I began to feel calmer. He had walked away and left me to look around on my own—certainly not the act of a desperate killer. My breathing steadied gradually as I went over Liam's words to me.

Like so many others, I had seen the movie *McLintock*, with John Wayne and Maureen O'Hara. I had gone with a boyfriend to see the film a couple of years back. I had been surprised by how turned on I'd become at the two spankings shown in the film. It opened up a deep yearning within me; I felt foolish and embarrassed about these feelings. After all, here we were in a new era of the emancipation of women; I mean, women were burning their bras for goodness sake! I thought that I had successfully tamped down my baser feelings and was doing rather well as a liberated woman of the sixties. However, my emotions were running amok since Liam had made *that* threat. It proved that I was still turned on by the whole dominant male role thing. I had dated a couple English men, young and a bit nerdy. I had pushed them and pushed them, behaving badly, y'know turning up late for dates, starting stupid arguments. However, instead of the spanking that I was pushing for, they simply dumped me and moved on to sweeter natured girls. It had been a long time since I had dated anyone, after all, where are you going to find a cowboy in England? Let alone a boy who is self-assured enough to spank his date? Well, you're just not going to are you, not in England in the sixties. I sighed, swallowed and licked my dry lips. I opened my eyes and began to look about me with interest.

The area left of the entrance was an open plan. An old-fashioned black pot-bellied stove stood at one side. On closer inspection, I saw it was a modern reproduction. A solid cedar wood circular table and chairs stood close by. The wall opposite the doorway was studded with coat hooks, below which ran a long wooden bench. It looked a typical bunkhouse, reminiscent of times gone by. There was an object that resembled a frying pan hanging on one of the coat hooks but, when I took a closer look, it was made of leather, some kind of table tennis bat maybe? I hung the thing back up and went back to exploring the bunkhouse. It was finished to a very high standard and the whole building was fairly new and solid. A corridor ran to the right of the entrance with spacious rooms off on either side. I walked over to the first door, a heavy wood affair with a solid black latch. It was a double bedroom en-suite, charmingly rustic but still luxurious. The only picture in the large room was an enormous framed photograph of a bucking bronco caught against a spectacular sunrise that hung above the bed. I studied the picture with an amateur eye and was struck by the phenomenal power of the subject. It was truly a thing of beauty. I wondered who the photographer was. I found that every bedroom had one large, original framed photograph, hung above the bed. Each framed photo was completely unique. Whoever had taken these shots knew what they were doing. My favourite was of a young cowgirl silhouetted against a cornflower-blue sky. Her head was thrown back; her glossy, sable hair flowed down over her shoulders, spilling to her waist. Her hat hung below her shoulders, one arm was raised high and she was pouring a canteen of water over her face; blue eyes half closed in private bliss, as rivulets of water cascaded over her face. Each droplet of water shone like a jewel, each one suspended in time, reflecting a mini rainbow of colour. It was eerie to stand and stare at my own mirror image, enlarged, framed, and hanging on a wall. It was Claire, of course. I stood and contemplated the stunning photograph for a long, long while. I was captivated by the beauty of the shot and fascinated by our mutual likeness. I wondered who had taken these amazing photographs. Finally I left, quietly closing and locking the door behind me. A deep melancholy enveloped me and I wanted to get back to the house as quickly as I could. The diary awaited me and I felt ready to unlock any secrets that it might hold. After locking up the bunkhouse, I scanned the area for Liam O'Donnell. I wanted to return the keys but there was no sign of him or anyone else, so I pocketed them and headed back the way I had come.

Sarah awaited me on my return. She shooed me into the living room where a welcoming fire roared and crackled in the hearth. Presently she brought in a tray of tea and homemade muffins. "Now then, you sit yourself down there and have your tea in peace."

She paused and then asked, "Claire dear... I wondered, did you know that your father was going to cancel next Saturday?"

"Saturday?" I whispered using my fake drawl. *Now what for goodness sake, what on earth was happening on Saturday?*

"Aye, he said because of your er, accident he felt it inappropriate to hold a party. What do you think? I mean to say… we have a party on your father's birthday every year… it's a tradition so it is!"

I could well understand my father not wishing to celebrate after the death of his daughter. However, since nobody here *knew* of Claire's death, people would think it odd indeed if the party were not held as usual.

"Well, of course the party must go ahead as always!" I tried to sound indignant.

Sarah sighed with relief. "Och good, I hoped you would say so. I took it upon myself to start the ball rolling and Liam and his men are going to begin organising things tomorrow. Since you have lost your voice, it seemed much the best solution." Sarah leant over and patted my arm as she said this. "Is that okay with you, lassie? I have divided the tasks that require the use of the telephone between Kate and me and you had better talk to Liam about this year's theme... oh and the band arrangements."

"Yeah, of course, thanks, Sarah," I whispered, nodding enthusiastically. My heart missed a beat at the thought of any further dealings with Liam O'Donnell. Sarah, pleased with herself, sauntered away, humming gaily.

How was I to cope with an event where I would be expected to know everyone? Perhaps I could pretend to be completely drunk and call everyone *darling!*

Sarah appeared back at the door again. "Oh, and I quite forgot to tell you, your father is returning in the morning with Molly and Den. He said to tell you he's sorry and that they don't know anything. Does that make any sense to you? He assured me you would understand his meaning?"

Molly and Den... Who on earth were they? I realised that Sarah was waiting for a reply from me. She seemed to take my silence as disapproval, because she then added, "I know, I know, they have their own place in Vegas, so why do they keep coming down here? But you know, Claire dear, she is his wife and even though Dennis is no blood relation to you, he is still your stepbrother and he is very fond of you, despite the way you freeze him out all the while."

Wife... step brother? What the hell was going on—what sort of cheap trick was my father pulling? Luckily Sarah continued her chattering and that covered the fact I could not have spoken had I tried; I didn't know what to think.

I ran upstairs and found Jules. She had made an excellent job of the locks and I was relieved to know that I would sleep more easily that night.

I told her about my meeting with Liam and asked her to find out who the photographer was that had taken the wonderful pictures up on the bunkhouse walls. Jules looked coyly at me as she asked what I had thought of Liam. "Well, I wasn't going to say anything," I said, flushing, "but you won't believe this, he threatened to er, *spank me*!"

Jules threw back her head and laughed. "He's quite a dish—I wouldn't mind a trip over his knee... those girls always come around in the end; he's a born natural!"

"What girls?" I asked.

"The naughty girls, the ones that are sent here to reform, of course."

I gaped at her. "My father told me nothing at all about any of this!"

Jules sighed, "That man, I'm sorry, I know that he is your father an' all, but... really! Sit down and I'll explain how it all works. What happens is this; rich parents contact Liam at the ranch when their daughter's, or sometimes a son's, behaviour is out of control and ask that the ranch takes the brat on full-time. The teen is set boundaries and they have to work hard, each one is given daily chores to do. They work with the horses and so forth, for however long it takes to turn them around. They earn themselves privileges for good behaviour. Liam is in charge of that side of things, he doles out the discipline as and when it's required. Loss of privileges to begin with and then if they persistently re-offend, usually a paddling. There is always another adult present when a kid earns a punishment and it is entered into a discipline record book. The whole ranch reform thing pays really well and the demand for this type of hands-on, 'one to one' residential discipline care is growing fast."

Wow. "Ok-ay, I did not know that... does it work?" I asked curiously.

"Yup, seems to. My precinct sent a kid here last year and now she's settled in college and doing really well. We hear from her mom from time to time."

"Um, can I ask, what is a 'paddling'?"

Jules grinned. "A spanking with a paddle y'know?"

A vision of the brown leather bat like object that I had found hanging in the bunkhouse came to mind and I nodded my understanding. I didn't know what else to say, the concept was so new to me. Thinking about my father, I was angry that he'd neglected to share with me something as important as this about the ranch.

Jules knew that my father was married to Molly and she was amazed and extremely cross with him for not telling me about Molly or her son Dennis. Apparently, they had a house on the outskirts of Las Vegas. Dennis managed one of the Keedon Motels in Vegas, the only one that had a casino attached. She told me that Molly had met my father some ten years ago in New York. He had fallen for her in a big way and they had married after only two months. Dennis, Molly's son, had been working as a croupier in an Atlantic City casino. After Molly and my father married, Dennis began to work for his stepfather in the motel in Las Vegas. Although the house in Vegas was their married home, from what information Jules could glean from the staff, my father chose to spend more time here than there. Apparently, she had questioned him as to whether Molly would be in on the secret of my identity and he had said absolutely not. This alarmed me until Jules explained that he had said Molly could not keep secrets. So, another hurdle to be jumped, a stepmother and a stepbrother. Boy, I would give my father 'what for' when I next saw him.

Shutting myself into Claire's room, I retrieved the diary from where I had hidden it this morning, under the carpet behind my bed. With a sense of wonder, I began to read—it was as if Claire stood at my side talking to me. As I read, I had a strong sense of her presence.

'Daddy told me today that he had put Liam in charge of the tourists and the bad girls. Why when I am so confident of running the tourist side of things? I think he still sees me as his little girl. Just because I didn't go to

away to college, but stayed at home and went to the local one instead, does not mean I have any less maturity. I must find a way to convince him that I am ready to handle some of the ranch business.'

I read on down the pages, skimming them until I came to this. It was dated two years ago.

'What is Daddy up to… Dennis cannot run a casino! He is a sweet young man and by all accounts, was a competent croupier, but surely Daddy must see his limitations in trying to run a business? He has no business acumen and no head for figures at all! I must speak to Daddy and maybe to Dennis too.'

I read on, skipping entries here and there.

'It was my birthday today and Liam gave me a wonderful framed photograph of myself. He is a genius with that camera. The photo gave me a brilliant idea for the bunkhouses, I hope Liam will agree. He can act so proprietarily and be damn awkward at times. I was really touched by his present though because I know that, at times, I irritate him tremendously. Sometimes I think he might even forget himself and spank me!'

Ah, so Liam was the photographer. Hmm, hidden depths—so my sister was worried he'd spank her. I wasn't the only one worried about protecting her bottom! It occurred to me that our father might have spanked Claire as a child. I wondered what it felt like to be spanked, how much would it hurt? I shook myself out of my reverie and began to read again.

'Matt is such a hon. I know he really likes me but I don't know what it is. Although I like him, I don't really dig him.'

Interesting.

'He wants me to partner him at Leanne's birthday hoedown. Maybe I will.'

I carried on reading, then further on.

'Matt say's he loves me. I really do like him, but do I love him? I wish I could take last night back. He might have believed me then.'

What had happened that night, I wondered?

'Daddy and I aren't talking. He can be so stubborn at sometimes! I have told him I am worried about the figures and he threatens me with a spanking

for shouting at him just as if I'm some little kid still. Heck, he just needs to hear me out'.

What's this? So Claire *had* been spanked as a child. I panned back to find out more. The date was only six months ago. A tap on my door made me jump out of my skin. "Just a moment," I called, kicking myself for not remembering to whisper. I closed the diary, hurriedly stuffing it under the pillow out of sight. Luckily, when I opened the door it was my father. He looked sheepish.

"Hi, honey, I hear you already know about Molly."

"Hmm yes, and Dennis," I added coldly, tapping my foot and holding the door still.

"Nicky, hon', I'm sorry, I was selfish I know. It's just I thought you might think all these people a bit scary and not agree to come over and impersonate Claire."

"You are absolutely right and I am packing my things and leaving right now!" Childishly, I wanted to scare him.

"What? Darlin', no...Aw, honey, I'm sorry. I know that I should have told you about Molly, she isn't here very often you see, so… I thought it could wait awhile."

"Another incidental," I said, sarcastically.

"I guess." He either didn't get the sarcasm, or chose to ignore it.

Voices from downstairs drifted up to us. My father looked over his shoulder. "Can I come in… just for a moment, please?"

I drew back, holding the door wide so that he could enter. "Thanks," he said and sat down heavily on the bed. I shut the door but remained standing, my arms folded.

"I have told Molly and Den that you have lost a chunk of memory and may not recall either of them. I thought that might make it easier for you."

"Cool, thanks, but you should have told me about them."

"Yeah, I know… what can I say, I'm sorry, Nicky… forgive an old man?"

I snorted at that but nodded. There was little else I could do after all. "Why are you keeping my identity a secret from your own wife?"

"Molly just cannot keep secrets. She'd try real hard but she'd just have to tell so and so, in absolute confidence, of course. Then 'so and so' would tell 'so and so' and on it would go. No, our secret must remain between us, Jules obviously and Matt, who already knows. Have you seen him today by the way?"

"Matt no… but I did meet Liam O'Donnell."

"Did you now... and what did you make of him?"

I frowned. "Well, he's a good-looking guy. A bit threatening in his manner though, I thought."

"Threatening… O'Donnell… surely not?"

"Well, I found him… somewhat… strange at any rate." I paused. "Do you know of any reason he may have disliked or even hated Claire?"

My father looked thoughtful. "No, not really, *not hated,* at any rate. Claire was taking charge of the dude side of things, you know, the books mainly, whereas, up to now, Liam had been running the whole show. Perhaps he felt a bit resentful. I guess I hadn't thought about that. It just seems so impossible to think of Liam ever hurting anything, let alone *killing.* I have to say… I don't think he's our guy."

"Yeah, but the police think it was someone from the ranch."

"'I know, I know they do. I just can't believe *any* of our people are capable of murder. Until that day, I would have trusted anyone here with my daughter's life."

I sat next to him on the bed and took his hand in mine. "I keep forgetting how you must be feeling. Are you okay?"

He looked at me and I could see the raw pain of loss in his eyes.

"I pretend," he said, quietly.

"Pretend?" I queried.

"Yeah, that nothing has happened—that you truly *are* Claire.

It's only when we talk like this it becomes real and… well, I just… can't bear it."

"Oh, Dad." I swallowed hard and reached out, hugging him.

He leaned into me and returned the hug. We sat quietly together for a moment. He broke the silence first.

"That's the first time you've called me Dad you know… as yourself I mean, not as Claire. I am so glad you're here with me… my Nicky." I nodded and just before I could speak, there was a knock at the door. My father jumped up and opened the door a crack. "Ah, it's you, come on in." Jules came into the room, throwing her jacket onto the chair.

"Hi there, Mr. Keedon, has Claire told you about the curtain thing last night?"

My father turned and fixed me with a gimlet eye. "No, she has not."

I stared back at him and shrugged. "It's all cool and I didn't want to worry you," I told him.

"Not worry? Hell, I'm worrying all the goddamn time, you ridiculous girl! Now tell me, what is this 'curtain thing'?"

Jules explained and I shifted uncomfortably under my father's furious gaze.

"You weren't going to tell me any of this, were you?" He was glaring at me from under his bushy brows.

I shrugged.

"Nicky, you will tell me everything, however small, that occurs from now on… do you understand me?!"

I nodded, my face flushed with embarrassment. He may be my father but I barely even knew him and here he was yelling at me, the way any regular Dad yells at his kid. I relaxed and felt a warm glow building inside of me at the thought.

"Nicky are you listening to me? If I hear one more thing you haven't told me about, then big as you are, I promise that, as your father, I will put you over my knee—you got that?"

I was so embarrassed by his words. *What was it that made the men out here want to spank their women at every provocation?* However I surprised him by jumping up and hugging him. He stood stiffly, still angry at me. "Of course I promise to tell you everything that happens from now onwards," I told him, pecking his cheek. He relaxed but looked surprised at my ready capitulation but, obviously gratified, he gave mc a massive hug back.

"Okay-okay, it's just I'm *responsible* for putting you in this situation and I just want to protect you is all."

"I know, Daddy, it's all cool. I understand," I said, smiling gently at him.

He harrumphed and reached for the door handle. "All right, enough, let's go eat."

Jules put her hand on the door. "Just a moment, Mr. Keedon, about this party you normally hold on your birthday."

"Yup."

"I think it should go ahead as normal."

"No. Sorry. I cannot celebrate under the circumstances."

"I understand that," Jules said, gently. "However, it will look very odd to the killer if you don't carry on as usual. Nicky is meant to be Claire, why then would you cancel the event?" My father looked at her thoughtfully.

"Mmm, yes, I suppose it would look odd. It is supposed to be held Saturday next. I'll speak to Sarah."

"Thank you, Mr. Keedon. It is important that you all behave as normally as possible. You know—using the same routines and so on."

"Yup, I realise that. Thank you, Jules. Come on then, let's go eat."

"I'll be right behind you," I called, before I dashed back into the room and hid the diary safely away for later.

6

Terror

Faces turned towards us as we entered the dining room. They gazed past my father and me, to where Jules stood. I realised, it was not I they took for the stranger in our midst… but Jules. I was just as they expected. I was Claire. I was the same as always and I must remember to behave as Claire. So did Claire usually kiss Molly and Dennis? I went towards Molly and smiled at her, she held out her cheek as if expecting an embrace thus making the decision to kiss easy for me. She was a tiny bird-like person with a pretty but over painted face, sharp eyes and carefully coiffured, fake copper coloured hair. We embraced briefly and she asked me how I was feeling. All the while, her eyes were fixed on Jules with open curiosity. I assured her of my well-being in a soft whisper and then half turned to introduce Jules as my therapist. Dennis, her son, was a tall man, slim and ginger haired. I wondered if perhaps my judgement of Molly's hair as fake was unjustified. Dennis gave me a friendly grin and reached out and hugged me fondly, "Hi, sis, been in the wars I hear... feeling okay now?"

I assured him that I was, "A-Okay!" in my usual whisper and he laughed at me in a teasing way. I liked him. I had not expected to be treated as a sister and I found it a pleasant surprise that he was so relaxed around me. My father patted my shoulder and grinned around the table at us. I think he was genuinely pleased to have his family meet me at last, even though they themselves didn't realise they were meeting *me*. I had forgotten that Claire was a vegetarian and was slightly disappointed to be served a pasta bake, while the others all tucked into Sarah's delicious smelling stew, beef in red wine sauce. Though my pasta was delicious, creamy and fragrant, the rich smell of the stew set me longing to taste some of the meat dinner. I was a complete hypocrite—I loved the meat experience—the chew, rich flavours—I just didn't agree with eating other species of mammal. I always feel so guilty about enjoying meat when the practice goes against what I believe.

The conversation flowed around me and, to my relief, it seemed that I was not expected to join in much, other than the odd nod and smile. I had my father to thank for that. He took the trouble to keep on adding to discussions that included me. "Just nod, Claire, don't try and talk. She must rest her voice… isn't that so, Miss Danker?"

"Oh absolutely, Mr. Keedon, the more Claire rests her throat, the quicker her voice will recover." I smiled gratefully at her for that.

"Claire?" It was Dennis. I turned and smiled at him across the table. "Can't you remember anything, any tiny little detail?"

I shook my head. "Sorry, no," I whispered.

"Den!" My father boomed warningly at him.

"Hey, I'm just curious. Seems real strange to me that you can't remember anything at all about such a terrible experience."

"Actually, it's not that unusual. People often forget things they would rather not recall. Claire's memory will return given time." I glanced at Jules gratefully. She smiled winningly at Dennis, Jules seemed to like him and either he had picked up on that, or the feeling was reciprocated. They flirted together throughout the rest of the meal and then went outside for some 'air' together before coffee. I excused myself too, expressing a desire for an early night and went upstairs to my room. I decided to have a bath, relax and plan the following day. I filled the bath using some of Claire's heavenly scented bath oil which stood on the side of the tub.

I was stretched out full-length in the bath, my eyes closed enjoying the sensation of the warm, sweet smelling water, when I noticed the light beyond my eyelids had suddenly darkened. Opening my eyes, I realised it was pitch black. Without warning, rough hands grasped me about the shoulders, fingers dug into my throat and my head was forced downwards beneath the water. I grappled with my assailant trying to prise their hands off me. It proved impossible since my attacker had on a pair of close fitting gloves that were so slippery I couldn't get a proper grip on them. I cursed myself for being so liberal with the bath oil and kicked and flailed uselessly. My lungs burned and I was becoming desperate. My eye sockets felt as though they would explode with pain. Someone was killing me and this was for real!

I knew I was about to die. I would if I didn't do something now. Frantically searching behind me, my hands hunted for anything to grab onto. My hand brushed up against something solid, the bottle of bath oil. I flailed about trying to get a grip on the neck of the bottle. Desperately floundering and slipping, my hand finally grasped the glass neck and lifting it high, I brought it down as hard as I could onto my attacker, wildly hitting out until I felt solid impact. It was a few seconds before I realised that the hands holding me down had released me and I was free. I burst upwards through the surface of the bath water gasping, filling my painful lungs with huge gulps of precious air. It was pitch black as I scrambled from the bath. I slapped at the wall trying to locate the light pull in the inky dark. Finally I had it and I was bathed in blessed light. I could see. I stumbled out into the bedroom but that room too was in darkness. I reached for the light switch and turned it on. The door was slightly ajar; otherwise the room was as I had left it moments before. Hurriedly, I closed and locked my bedroom door and reached for a towel. Then I sat on the bed and began to shake. I had nearly died. Claire had suffered the same suffocating pain that I had just done. The difference being that she *had* died. The awful desperate struggle for air, the burning in my chest, my own sister had died in just that way. Her killer was here, somewhere in this house at this very minute. I leapt up and patted my clothes, searching for the walkie-talkie, finding it I pressed it with a trembling figure. Where was Jules—was she inside the house? I dried quickly, pulling on the clothes I had taken off before my bath. "Come on, come on," I muttered urgently to myself as I fumbled into my clothes with difficulty.

After ten minutes had passed with no response to my walkie-talkie, I decided to go and find Jules or my father. I felt so unsafe that I needed a weapon for protection but after a fruitless search for something sharp, I gave up. I was partially relieved, not being certain that I could use such a thing. I decided to take a tin of hair spray with me; at least I could temporarily blind an attacker and so make good my escape.

The house was very quiet. Though I didn't find Jules, the question as to why my call had received no response became obvious when I saw the second walkie-talkie sitting in the middle of Jules's bed, light flashing to indicate my call. Closing the door, I descended the stairs cautiously. I crept into the dining room, by now deserted, leaving the lights switched off so I could observe outside without being seen. I could see the shadow of someone out of the window, across the yard towards the barn. I crept up to the side of the wall to the window, careful to stay within the darkness of the side of the frame. Nestled up against the curtains, I watched as a person crept along the wall of the barn. I couldn't tell if it were a man or woman, a few paces more and they would be caught in the light shining out from the porch, then I would know. Holding my breath, I waited to see who it would be. Suddenly the room was flooded with harsh light and I blinked in the sudden glare.

"Miss Scarlet in the dining room with the… whatever is that… my God, hairspray. Claire, you feeling okay?"

It was Dennis. He was standing in the doorway of the room. I nodded feebly and sat down on the nearest chair, promptly bursting into tears. Dennis was very kind and gentle with me, offering me his handkerchief and insisting that I have a glass of brandy.

My father appeared in the doorway. "Ah there you are, Den, gee, we thought you'd gone to France for the brandy, you've been gone for so long. N-Claire, what's happened?"

He crossed the floor and knelt at my side. "Honey?" I reached out and leaned into his big frame and he, in turn, gathered me close. "You're shaking girl. Den, what happened here?" he asked his step-son sharply.

"Nothing. I came in to fetch the brandy and found Claire here in darkness, looking out of the window." Dennis sounded aggrieved.

"That's all?"

"Sure. I don't know what's wrong with her. She was brandishing a can of hairspray, nerves I expect. She was real upset though, so I poured her a brandy, cheers, Claire." He lifted his own glass and took a drink.

I lifted my head, "Thanks, Dennis."

"Hey, you didn't whisper!" Dennis pointed out.

"Right—come on, young lady, bedtime for you!" My father spoke quickly to cover up my blunder. I nodded and we headed for the stairs. "Den, go tell your Mom what's happened and tell her I'll be right with her once I've settled Claire down for the night." He guided me with a large hand on my shoulder. Dennis saluted comically and went to find his mother.

Inside my room, my father shut the door firmly and locked it behind him. I flopped onto the bed shaking still. "Now, Nicky, tell me everything." He hunkered down in front of me and took my hands in his. "Tell me, child," he coaxed gently.

I took a shuddering breath. "Someone tried to drown me in the bath. They held me down under the water… they were choking me. Oh God, I know exactly how my sister died—how much she suffered... I"

"Goddamn it! Hush now, hey there, hey daddy's here, I'm right here!" He gathered me into his arms and rocked me. The tears finally came in a torrent and I sobbed out my fright. My father held me silently, stroking my hair back from my face before saying. "This has gone far enough. I'm gonna call this thing off right now. I don't know what I could have been thinking, risking your life this way!"

I pulled back from him, horrified, swabbing at my drenched face. "No, no you mustn't do that… we're getting close… don't you see?" I gripped his knee saying urgently, "Whoever killed Claire was in the house tonight—I have touched him—I have touched my sister's killer!"

My father reached into his pocket and bought out a clean white handkerchief and he mopped my face, finally holding the cloth to my nose. "Blow!" he ordered.

"Now then, Nicola, just you listen to me. I cannot take the risk of losing you too. I have lost one daughter and I refuse to let this go on until I lose you as well! Where the hell is Jules? Dammit, the woman's supposed to protect you! This is…"

As if on cue, there was a soft knock at the door and Jules whispered, "It's me, let me in." My father leapt up, unlocked the door and let Jules in.

One look at my face and Jules knew that something dreadful had occurred. My father filled her in briefly and she listened gravely until he had finished. Then she turned to me.

"I am so sorry about the walkie-talkie. I simply forgot to pick it up after I went to the bathroom." She paused but when I simply nodded, thinking it was a pretty amateur mistake to make, she continued. "Well one thing's for sure; it was someone on the ranch. I was outside watching the house and no one came in or out of either the front or side kitchen entrance. I didn't see or hear any vehicles either."

"Would you have heard a horse or someone on foot?" I asked her.

"Yeah, I think so. It was very quiet out there, but just maybe somebody on foot could have snuck around the back without me noticing them," she mused aloud.

"I think we should call this whole charade off right now!" my father said firmly.

Jules looked at him sharply. "Call it off… we are getting so close, Mr. Keedon."

My father butted in, "I know that but I won't lose another daughter! This has to end now!"

Jules pulled herself upright and glared at him. "With respect, Mr. Keedon, this whole plan was your idea. We warned you of the risks involved but you insisted on trying this. Well, now your idea is working, and I will only cry off the plan if Nicola wishes it."

Before either of them could argue further, I broke in. "Shut up both of you… I want to carry on. If *I decide* otherwise I'll let you both know!"

My father sighed, defeated. "Well, all right then, but I have a condition."

Jules and I waited. "Nicola and I will take a little trip after the party. There's somewhere special I'd like to take you to see, hon. We could do with a break from the awful stress of this and we can take time to get properly acquainted. I want to spend some quality time with my daughter. It will do you good to feel safe, for a little while at least."

Jules nodded. "I agree. What do you think, N-Claire?"

I nodded; it would be lovely to go away and spend time alone with my father, just the two of us.

He rubbed his hands together. "Right then, that's settled, but until we leave, I want you to sleep in here with Nicola, Miss Danker. Don't you leave her side for a single second you hear?"

"No," I said firmly, "that would just look odd."

"No it wouldn't, not if we say that this is the sort of scenario the doctor expected might happen. After all, that is why I am here to help you over the trauma of what has happened to you, all part of the therapy to help regain your voice."

"That's brilliant, Jules. I must admit I would feel a lot safer with you in here with me." I smiled gratefully at her.

A voice called from the stairs. "Coo-ee darlin'."

"Molly," my father muttered. "I'd better go tell them the line we're gonna use. You okay now, honey?" He looked at me anxiously.

"I'll be fine now that Jules is here. Thank you, Daddy." I stood up and we hugged.

He kissed my forehead. "My brave girl." He gazed at my face intently before leaving, gently closing the door behind him.

With Jules asleep on a 'put you up' bed across my door, I felt safe and I slept well. The following morning she de-briefed me about the events of the previous night. She asked me to shut my eyes and re-live the whole episode. I did as she asked. Jules stopped me at certain points and asked me to try and remember sounds and scents that might be important. I told her all that I could remember about the person who tried to drown me. "I am convinced my attacker was a man," I told her, my eyes shut as I relived that horrible moment.

"Why?" she asked.

"Perhaps the size of the hands holding me under in the water?"

"What else… could you smell him?"

"Yes, the smell of lemons, faint but definitely citrusy"

"Anything else? Did you grab any clothing, anything about the texture of the clothes?"

"Mmm, whoever it was wore kitchen gloves." I opened my eyes triumphantly.

Jules nodded. "Okay, good. We don't know that our attacker was male but the hands were large and had gloves on. Claire, you might recognise the citrus scent on someone at a most unexpected time; I want you to be prepared for that.

"I'm cool!" I nodded, excited at the prospect.

Jules smiled thinly. "You might find your reaction surprising. You may feel you want to attack this person or maybe you will feel overwhelmed and tearful. The thing is you must keep your emotions under control. Give *nothing* away. It won't be easy you know… not after last night."

I nodded, chewing my bottom lip anxiously. "What happens if I do, you know, crack up?"

"Don't worry. I will be close by; I'll step right in and arrest them. Now let's get some air. Have you visited that horse of yours yet?"

"No, I'm not really very good with horses," I confessed.

"Well you're supposed to be brilliant with them, so let's go make a big fuss of… Sable, isn't it?"

I laughed, "No, it's Sasha—yeah, I'll take some mints for her, 'cupboard love', it always works with dogs."

7

Courage

The problem was that when we arrived at the stables, none of the horses had their names written up on their stalls as I had assumed they would be.

"Oh lord, so which one is Sasha?" Jules asked, looking along the row of stalls. On hearing us approach, the occupants had hung out eager heads over their stable doors, blowing softly and nodding enthusiastically for our attention.

"I have absolutely no idea." I shrugged helplessly, looking down the line of equine hopefuls.

"All right, well then, we have to rely on the horse recognising you. Walk along slowly and see if one of them reacts." Jules gave me a gentle shove forward and I slowly wandered up the stable looking at each horse in turn to see if any one of them recognised me. Just when I was thinking what a total waste of time this idea was, a horse near the end of the row whickered loudly and pawed the ground. I hurried over to the stall. A lovely pale honey coloured horse with a milky coloured mane was swinging her head to and fro; I just knew this one was Sasha. The mare put her nose out and I held my hand out to her. Ears pricked forwards, she sniffed at my hand delicately and threw back her head whinnying loudly. I jumped and started backwards slightly. I stumbled into something solid behind me.

"Orf… hey, whoa there, girl!"

"Gosh I am so sorry!" I said automatically and then blushed crimson when I remembered that I shouldn't be talking and certainly not sounding so very English. It was Liam. His clear intelligent eyes studied me with interest.

"Howdy, Miss Claire. Sasha's acting kinda weird around you today." We both turned and watched as Sasha pawed the ground and shook her mane, nodding her head up and down crossly.

"She probably remembers the last time she saw me when we had our—er, accident." This time I remembered to whisper and drawl.

"Sure is strange how your voice comes and goes like that," he said mildly, shaking his head and giving me a searching look with those bright eyes of his. I glanced around in panic for Jules. She was seemingly engrossed in the horse tack hanging on the wall on the other side of the barn. Shit, why didn't she come over here and rescue me?

I realised that Liam had spoken and was waiting for me to reply. "Sorry? I missed that," I whispered. Liam nudged back his hat and gave me a long look. I squirmed and felt the tell-tale warmth of yet another blush creeping up my neck. What was it about this guy that made me so gauche and unreasonably angry with him every time I laid eyes on him?

"Have you no work to be getting on with, O'Donnell? There's a party to organise for next Saturday—I'd have thought you'd have plenty to do!" I hissed nastily at him. He gave me a strange assessing look and then his face broke into grin and he nodded agreeably.

"You sure are a different girl since you went and banged that pretty head of yours. If you don't get that sweet personality of yours back real soon, I can help you find it—upside down across my knee—I mostly find a toasty butt sweetens a little girl up real fine! So, shall we call this 'strike one'?"

I flushed to the tips of my ears and was so flustered all I could do was look down at my toes. Liam spoke again as if nothing untoward had been said "So, Claire, what theme do you want for the hoe-down this year?"

Blankly, I muttered, "Hoe-down?" I was still in shock, vividly picturing myself upside down getting a toasty bottom.

"Yeah, your daddy's birthday gig."

I thought quickly. "Well, er, how about Mexican, we didn't have that last year did we?" I asked him.

"Nope, good idea, Mexican it is then, any other ideas?"

I nodded, "How about Chinese paper lanterns and lots of colour. Oh, and a few big potted cacti dotted around."

"Okay, I'll get on to it right away." I thanked him and wished he would go away; he made me nervous.

"D' you want Sasha tacked up? I'll do her for you, if'n you've forgotten how what with your accident an' all."

I spun around and turned my back on him, saying haughtily over my shoulder, "No thanks, Liam, I am quite capable of saddling my own horse, thank you very much. You get on back to your chores… after all, don't you have rather a lot to do before next Saturday?"

Liam shrugged. "Please yourself, princess. Sure is strange, your voice works one minute and not the next." He wandered over to Jules and started to chat with her while taking down various pieces of tack and examining them. I turned to the stall and gulped when I saw all the harnesses, now what had I let myself in for? What was it about that man that made me behave in such a foolish way whenever I was around him? Then it struck me. I stood stock still. I felt as though someone had suddenly dowsed me in icy water. What had Jules told me only an hour ago—I would probably feel strong anger or emotion around the man who had attacked me—that's how I would know him—so it must be Liam! It had to be him. However, I had to be certain. How could I tell whether he was my sister's killer?

"Having trouble over there, Miss Claire?" Liam's lazy voice called over. I ground my teeth and turned to face him, a false smile plastered across my face.

"I've changed my mind I just don't feel up to riding today." Once again, my whisper was more of a hiss.

Liam's grin vanished and he strode over to me. "Hey now, that's no good. If'n you take a fall, you know the rule—you climb right back up there and get on with it. Otherwise the fear stays with you. You should know that, Claire." He called me Claire, without the preceding and mocking 'Miss.' Startled by his earnestness, I found myself nodding dumbly in agreement. He spun around and fetched the tackle and saddle. I hesitated for a moment, gaining courage and then with a deep breath opened the stall and held out one of the mints for Sasha to take. She put her head forward and blew on my hair, before her soft velvet nose lowered to my outstretched hand and, with soft nibbling lips, she gently took the proffered treat. Pleased, I reached up and patted her neck. Liam opened the stall wider and stood aside as Sasha walked out and stood as gentle as a lamb while Liam saddled her for me. I watched as he moved his hands over her flanks, all the while talking soothingly to her in his deep, treacly drawl. I shivered and looked away. Jules caught my eye and grinned. She had tacked up her own horse very efficiently and was waiting for us.

"Will you join us, Liam?" she called over. I glared and shook my head slightly at her, rolling my eyes to convey my displeasure. She grinned back and mouthed, "What?"

I tossed my hair crossly and turned back to Liam, who was intent on tightening the girth and hadn't noticed our exchange. "As much as I'd like to ride with you girls, I have much too much to do today as Miss Claire so kindly pointed out," he replied, a small smile playing about his mouth.

"Oh what a shame… another time then," I hissed quickly, smugly pleased. Liam looked up at me, eyes narrowed, looking at me searchingly. Then he straightened up, still watching me. I felt the start of another blush, what the hell was the matter with me?

"I don't suppose you'd like to come with me tomorrow when I go to fetch the tables and chairs from old Harry's place? I could do with the extra help," he asked. I must have looked confused for he added, "The party, next Saturday, you know? Harry borrowed our trestle tables for his New Year's party remember?"

While I dithered, Jules stepped up eagerly. "Sure, we'd be glad to help," she said firmly. Then she added quickly, before I could spoil her plan, "Come on, Claire, mount up—let's go!" She swung herself into her saddle with ease. I, on the other hand, had not ridden a horse since the age of thirteen. I placed a foot into the stirrup and hopped about like a complete and total idiot.

Liam watched, his brow furrowed. "Hey there, Claire, take it easy girl!" He grabbed Sasha's reins and held her still. I hung onto the saddle and watched as he dipped under Sasha's head and came towards me. He hunkered down and clasped his hands together. "Okay, now try again." I was beetroot red with mortification by now but I obediently placed my foot in his joined hands and levered myself astride Sasha.

"Thanks, Liam," I whispered.

He gave me a grin. "You're a real brave girl, Claire. Only fear could affect you mounting badly that way. I admire your guts, getting back in the saddle when you're obviously terrified, well done!"

He was right there, I was very terrified. I smiled nervously and turned Sasha to follow Jules out of the stables. We walked the horses out of the corral and onto the pasture. I turned to check no one was in earshot and I saw Liam leaning against the barn watching us. I lifted an arm and waved. He didn't wave in reply and for some reason that irked me. "I think it's him," I said.

Jules looked at me in surprise. "Liam… nah!"

"Yes!" I insisted.

"You're attracted to him and that is what rattles you."

"I am so *absolutely not* attracted to him… whatever gave you that idea?"

"Shut up! You're supposed to whisper! I'll bet he heard you, yelling at me like that."

"I did not yell. Oh for goodness sakes, do you really think he heard me?" I slowly twisted around in the saddle to see but, thankfully, Liam had disappeared from sight.

Jules laughed. "You see, I was right, you do like him!"

"I think he's the one—you know, the killer!" I insisted again.

"Okay, why?"

"You remember you warned me I might feel some anger and emotion when I met the killer and that I would sense it was him? Well, I feel furious whenever I'm around him."

Jules studied me seriously. "Okay, it's possible, but from what I witnessed back there, seems to me jus' that you kinda fancy him, hon', and you are embarrassed by your feelings and became angry, more with yourself than with him."

I reflected on her words. Could it be that, I wondered. "I am sure I never behave like that with men I find attractive!" I protested.

"Well, spending time with him tomorrow is a real good idea because you will be able to sort out how you feel about him. Land sakes, remember to whisper will you?"

"Must we go with him tomorrow? I feel so uncomfortable with him," I wailed.

"Yes, Claire, we must. The only way to sort out how you feel is to spend time with him." She smiled at me to soften her words. "It'll be okay, I'll be there too."

I sighed sulkily, realising Jules had made her mind up and to argue would be futile. "Oh very well if you insist."

"I do. Now where shall we head for? Say, can you gallop?"

"I can ride, I'm just rusty," I assured her.

"Let's go then!" Boy, did she go! She left me in her dust. I tightened my knees, Sasha and I were off, racing through scenery I'd only seen in westerns on the television set back home. It was wonderful—and so much better in reality!

The wind lifted my hair and Sasha cantered swiftly and true. I felt like I was flying.

When we finally pulled up, both laughing and out of breath, I gazed at the rugged beauty all around me and my eyes filled with sudden tears. My sister had known and loved this country, this was her home. She had sat here, perhaps in this very spot as I did now. She had ridden every inch of this land and she should be here now enjoying all of this. Instead she was laid out, cold and dead in a morgue. I shook myself out of deep reverie as I realised that Jules was speaking to me.

"... and race you back!" She turned her horse and was away. I scanned the view one last time before following her in hot pursuit.

Later, Jules and I enjoyed a salad lunch; everyone else was out. I decided to continue reading Claire's diary. I ensured my door was locked and settled down at the desk. The curtains lifted in the breeze and I reached up to shut the window. As I did so, I noticed Matt standing in the shadow of the barn watching the house. I waved to him but he was looking elsewhere and didn't notice me. I frowned and sat back down pondering. Perhaps I should be more suspicious of Matt as the killer; after all, he had found Claire hadn't he? The police had questioned him and released him but was that purely due to lack of evidence? Surely he was the most logical suspect given the circumstances. I sat motionless for some moments thinking it all through.

I glanced down at the diary, my eyes scanning down the pages until I came to the last entry Claire had made, the day before her death.

'I don't know what to do. Everything is such a mess and Daddy won't listen to me about the figures. We aren't even talking properly anymore. Now

on top of everything else, Matt has proposed for real. Why couldn't we have just carried on as we were? He knows how I feel—what a mess!'

I re-read the entry twice and still it didn't make a lot of sense. I flicked back a page.

'Had a huge row with Daddy today about the figures, he won't hear me at all. I wonder if I should have left home after college like all my friends did. He doesn't seem to see me as an adult yet, despite my age. Surely he sees the success I have made of the dude side of the business. He must trust my judgement on this! So why won't he believe me when I tell him about the inaccuracies that I have found? We always had such a good relationship but lately he is shutting me out. I think I'll apply to a couple of advertisements I've seen for business managers in other states. Perhaps we need some distance. It would kill me to leave here but maybe just the threat of leaving would be enough to change his mind.'

I sat thoughtfully; so there was a rift between our father and Claire. Why had he not told me about that? Then there were the discrepancies that Claire had found. It sounded like the dude ranch needed some investigation. Again Liam sprung to mind. It seemed that I always came back to Liam. I scrolled back further but all I read were domestic entries and Claire's personal shopping requirements. At that point, Jules knocked on my door and called out that it was time for supper. I had no choice but to hide the diary away yet again.

8

Stoicism

The following morning, Jules and I were up early before the rest of the household were stirring. We made ourselves hot coffee and rolls for the journey and waited for Liam to collect us from the front of the house.

It was very cold and a sparkling frost covered the ground. I wore a thick dusty pink woollen polo sweater that had been Claire's as well as my new jeans. I made myself snug in a chunky sheepskin jacket that I found hanging in the closet downstairs. I had no idea who it belonged to but I suspected due to the fit, that it had been Claire's. There were knitted gloves stuffed into the pocket and I was grateful for their added warmth. Jules was dressed similarly in jeans, a shirt and sweater topped by a thick felted jacket and scarf. Her hands were bare and red from the cold already. "Have you any gloves with you?" I asked her, concerned.

"I'll be fine. We don't want Liam to leave without us. He'll be here soon, I'm okay."

"Look," I said, "you run and fetch them and I'll watch for Liam, he will wait for you."

"I don't know," she replied. She was hesitant and undecided. "I hate leaving you on your own, even for a second."

I was gratified. It was nice to feel someone was caring for me. If the truth was told, I felt a little let down by my father. Oh, he said all the right things, but his absent behaviour left a lot to be desired. "Ah, here he is," Jules said.

An ancient blue pickup was rattling down the drive towards the house.

"Is this your old banger?' I asked him, once Jules and I were seated inside.

"Old banger? I'll have you know this here is the work-horse of pickups, a Chevrolet Apache. My dad had one of these babies and I always promised myself one. In a bar one night, a fella asked if anyone wanted to buy his Chevy and the rest, as they say, is history. We were destined for one another, weren't we baby?" He patted the steering wheel lovingly.

"The only important thing is does the heater work?" Jules asked, her teeth chattering.

"Sure thing… can't you feel it?" Liam put his hand over the grill. "Yeah, it's definitely on," he confirmed.

Jules and I glanced at each other and she grimaced. "Here." I peeled off my gloves and gave them to her. "We'll share."

"Thanks," she said with real gratitude and pulled them on.

"Funny how your voice comes and goes like that," Liam said, eyes straight ahead watching the road.

I started and was about to reply, when I felt Jules's hand on my arm. She gave a warning squeeze. "Liam, how long will it take to get there do you reckon?" she asked as a distraction.

"Maybe a couple of hours, no more, maybe we'll stop at Jim's for a bite first."

"Jim's?" Jules asked.

"Yeah, he runs a diner half way to Harry's place, best steak n' fries around. So who's hungry?"

I spoke, remembering to whisper. I even tried my sexy drawl.

"We've hot coffee and rolls for our return journey later, would yer like some then, Liam?" Crumbs, I sounded more Irish than American.

"That'd be good. Hey, Claire, your voice is real strange. You must have knocked your head for sure, so how's your memory doing?"

Jules and I exchanged another frantic look. This time I replied, "It's really weird, I remember some things but others have just gone. My voice does come and go but the doc thinks that I might have banged the cerebral part of my brain that deals with speech."

"Hmm, seems to me it's more of a shock kinda thing." Liam glanced at me and gave me a smile. "You'll get back to normal when you're good and ready, you can't push these things."

I was touched and relieved; he didn't suspect a thing after all. "You sound as though you know what you're talking about," I said, seriously.

He was silent for a few minutes and then started to speak again in a low voice. "I'm a psychologist. My sister once had a bicycle accident and suffered headaches afterwards. When they started she wouldn't go to the doc'. She insisted it was part of the healing process. It wasn't, of course. It was a cerebral bleed and she died in her sleep. The doctors on your case are doing the right thing, giving you a nurse twenty-four seven. Of course, our health insurance then was no great shakes. You're real lucky, Miss Claire, your daddy can pay. Hey listen though, you get headaches you tell Jules here straight away okay?"

I was moved by his speech, the longest one I had heard Liam make so far and I was intrigued. I cleared my throat. "Um, thanks, Liam, I'll remember that. I'm sorry about your sister, it must have been a terrible shock for you and your parents." He nodded but said nothing more. Jules met my eyes and raised her eyebrows before taking in the view once more.

Jim's restaurant, Steak and Fries, lived up to expectation. I only had Jules's word to go on for that as, much to my disgust, Liam had kindly ordered egg and fries for me, remembering that I was a vegetarian. Would I ever get to taste a large, juicy American steak I wondered as I tucked into my very rubbery eggs? I glanced across at Liam to find his eyes on me. He immediately grinned, making no attempt to look away and I found myself smiling shyly back. "You've probably told me before about your family, Liam, but I've no recollection of it. Where is it you come from?"

"Wyoming and no, I don't think I ever did tell you 'bout my folks. They had a farm. My great-great-grandfather bought the land after he and his wife left Ireland at the start of the famine in 1845. Land was cheap over here then and he knew farming. He made a success by using the land diversely, crops, cattle and even hogs. I grew up on the family farm but I moved to Denver when I was thirteen to live with my aunt. My uncle died, and since they had no kids, she was real lonely. My mother was ill at the time and had to go into hospital for an operation. She needed recovery time afterwards, and to lessen her load, my father sent me to stay with my aunt." He stopped and took a mouthful of food.

"That must have been real hard on you. What was wrong with your mother? Oh! I'm sorry, maybe I shouldn't have asked that."

"No, no, that's okay. Mom had breast cancer and she had to have a breast removed. She's alive an' well and living proof you can beat the big C." He smiled at us both.

"Did you want to stay on in Denver after she was well again?" Jules asked.

"Yeah, I did for a while. I was settled in school and my aunt was well off. It made a change from constant chores and being the only kid in school with second-hand clothes." He saw the look on my face and laughed. "What can I say? I was shallow then, most kids are at that age."

"Not anymore?" I teased.

"I hope not," he said, seriously.

"Did you have any other brothers or sisters?" Jules asked.

"Nope jus' the one sister, Jessie was older than me. She and Mom were real close. Jessie was a big help when Mom got sick, you know nursing her an' running the house and all. Mom took it real hard when Jessie died after her bicycle accident."

"Is it strange when you go back to visit home?" I asked, curious now about this man.

"Yeah, kinda I suppose. I guess I feel I don't belong in either place now. That's why I took this job, you know? My own destiny centred on another State, exciting stuff," he grinned with that sexy, wicked smile, "even though it upset your dreams, kitten."

I wasn't quite sure what he meant until I remembered what I had recently read in Claire's diary so I assumed it had something to do with being in charge with the dude side of the ranch.

"Oh, I don't mind, after all, it won't be long before I take over the sole running of the whole kit and caboodle!" I said, unable to resist baiting him.

Liam turned his head and flashed a teasing grin at me. "Well now, darlin', from what your daddy tells me, that day will never come!" I scowled at him and wondered what my father had actually said.

"Hey, don't you look at me like that, angel. I can't help it if your Pa's dead against you burning your bra!" He chuckled and I stared at him in amazement. Was he right—was my father a male chauvinist? It made sense as to why he gave no credence to Claire's warnings. What had she found out? I vowed to spend however long it took me to read her diary until I found out the answer.

Back in the truck, Jules and Liam sang an awful rendition of an Elvis song. They murdered the tune and left me shaking with mirth; especially Liam's deep drawling *"I'm in lurr-ve... I'm all shook up... yeah... hey... hey."*

We were driving up a winding road with a steep drop to one side. I was engrossed with the spectacular views, when a car suddenly appeared, speeding around the corner in front of us. It fish-tailed out of control, ending up on the wrong side of the road and heading straight towards us. Liam wrenched the wheel over and the pickup lurched suddenly towards the drop. I screamed. The other car missed our truck by a hair's breadth but instead of stopping, the driver continued on his way. Liam struggled to straighten the truck as it swerved out of control, heading towards the road edge; we veered, tipped and careened out of control on the downward incline. We bounced sickeningly against rocks, ever onwards, descending the steep slope until the truck came to a bone jarring halt, our fall broken by a bushy coppice of small trees. Dazed, I lay twisted in my seat. I turned my head slowly to look at Jules who was slumped by my side. She had blood trickling down the side of her face; she was white and her eyes were shut.

I tried to say her name but nothing came out. I must have fainted because I don't remember any more until I heard a name called urgently over and over again, "Claire, come on open your eyes, Claire, Claire!"

What was my name? Oh yeah—Nicola—so why was someone calling me Claire?

"Come on now wake up," then a whisper, "Nicky, Nicky wake up now."

I opened my eyes. It was Jules, her poor face gory with blood and her nose was bleeding. I turned my head to look at Liam; he had a large bruise on his forehead and a scratch on his cheek. I lifted my hand and touched it with a fingertip, gently. "Poor, Liam, oh dear, he's spoiled his handsome face," I said dreamily.

"Claire," Jules said again.

"What? No, Nicky—I am Nicola." I nodded to emphasise the point.

"Yes, I do know that," Jules spoke gently, "but you are pretending to be Claire remember?"

I shook my head. "No, my head aches."

Jules looked anxiously at me. "I'm going to take a look at Liam now, all right?" She scrambled out of the truck and ran around to the driver's side.

My memory slowly returned and I began to remember where we were.

"Will he be okay?" I glanced anxiously at him, he seemed to be still unconscious.

"I must try to move him. I need your help, Claire, there's the risk of fire. We must get him out of the truck. Do you understand me? How's your head feel?"

I reached up and rubbed my forehead, it did feel sore and I was very dizzy. "It's a bit painful but otherwise I'm okay, I think. Give me a hand to get straight and I'll help you with Liam." Jules reached in and helped me to sit up properly. Luckily my legs seemed to be in working order and I gingerly climbed out of the truck. My legs were stiff and painful though. My shoulder hurt like hell but otherwise I thought I was all right and, I guessed, extremely lucky to be alive.

"How are you doing?" Jules asked, she had her arm around me, supporting me as I took a step.

"Um, just bruised I think."

"Right, I'm going to climb into the back of the truck and fetch the tarp. Then I'll go in on the passenger side and see if I can slide Liam back. Can you go around to the driver's side and see if you can free his legs? We'll slide him out of the driver's door if we can and onto the tarpaulin. Then we can drag him away from the truck." I nodded and shuffled over to the driver's side. Liam's legs seemed to be okay and I was able to lift first one and then the other leg out. Jules took each leg from me and laid them gently along the passenger seat. I pulled and twisted his body so that his back was to the driver's door and I was supporting him under his arms, his head resting back against my shoulder. He didn't stir throughout. While I supported Liam, Jules had fetched the tarpaulin from the back of the truck and spread it out on the ground behind where I stood. Jules then squeezed in beside me and supported Liam beneath his other arm. "Ready?" asked Jules, "on the count of three; one, two and *three!"* Between us, we managed to drag Liam out and down onto the tarpaulin.

Jules knelt beside him and methodically checked him over. I clambered into the battered truck and pulled out two blankets. "I don't think there are any broken bones," Jules muttered. I bent stiffly and covered him in the blankets, tucking them in around him, making Liam as warm as possible. "We need to pull him away from the truck in case of fire," Jules instructed, "but first I need to support his head." She took off her jacket and stripped off her sweater, pulled the jacket back on and then wrapped the sweater around Liam's neck and head, careful to keep his neck straight. We each held a corner of the tarpaulin above his head and pulled carefully, holding it high, so that Liam's head was not bumping along the stony ground. We managed to pull him some distance from the truck onto a grassy and reasonably flat piece of land. I flopped down beside Liam and tucked him up as snugly as I could with just two blankets. I gazed down the slope; tall dark spruce trees grew close together.

Were there wolves in those trees I wondered, trying to see in between the dark trunks and into the grey shadows beyond?

Jules came over to me and placed Liam's rifle on the ground beside me. "What's that for?" I squeaked with alarm.

"Your protection," she stated baldly, "do you know how to use one of these?"

I shook my head negatively.

"Right, well... here's the food and flask. I should be back in two or three hours."

I sat up straight. "What do you mean?"

"I am going to make my way back to Jim's steak house for help."

"No-No-No," I pleaded. "You cannot leave me alone here! I don't know how to use the damn gun or anything! What about wolves?" I tried to stand and failed, miserably falling back to the ground with a nasty jolt. My back and hip muscles were in spasm and very painfully so.

"Hey, it'll be okay! You'll be just fine! What's all this about wolves?" Jules actually grinned at me.

"Don't you dare laugh, there *might* be wolves!" I was cross with her mocking me.

"Yeah well, somehow I doubt it. Look I'll show you how to use the rifle." She picked the rifle up and held it out to me. The barrel pointing towards the tress, safely away from us both. "Okay, so you release the safety lock, point and pull the trigger back gently to fire. Oh, and never, *ever* point a loaded gun at someone. Well not unless you *want* to shoot them of course. Look, I have to go, Claire. Liam needs a doctor and it will only take me two to three hours, tops."

"But you're hurt as well. Perhaps we should all wait here together. They will worry about us at The Plomosa when we don't arrive back; surely someone will come looking for us."

"Liam might need medical attention before then, Claire. No, I do have to go. You'll be just fine, it won't be any hardship to cuddle up with Liam and keep him warm! I promise not to be too long."

"All right then," I agreed sulkily. I was scared and confused; I wondered if I had some sort of concussion. "Go carefully, and good luck," I added as optimistically as I could.

"Thanks, Claire… Nicola. I promise to be back by dark okay? By-ee." And with that, she turned and strode off, leaving me alone out in the wilderness, with an unconscious man and a rifle I didn't know how to shoot.

"Great!" I grumped aloud. I turned at looked at Liam but,

thankfully, he was breathing normally and looked fairly peaceful. There was no way I could sleep. Someone had to keep a look out. A little while later what did I do in the face of adversity? Promptly fell asleep.

WHEN I AWOKE it was twilight. Where the devil was Jules? Pieces of fluff were dusting my face. Drowsily I lifted a hand and brushed away what I thought were threads of cobweb or something. My hand encountered tiny, icy wet droplets of snow. Looking up at the sky I saw it was heavy with deep grey-mauve clouds. I glanced at Liam; he hadn't moved. Reaching out a hand I felt his brow. He was cold but underneath the blankets he felt warm. At least he was still alive. My gaze moved down the slope, into the shadows between the tall dark trees. So secret and threatening, creatures could lurk within their dark, sinister protection. I shuddered and spoke aloud, trying to dispel the silent eeriness surrounding me. "Just great, here I am, just survived an attempt to strangle me and now I'm about to die of exposure in the wilderness. Well I tell you what, *I won't die...* do you hear that, you evil things in the forest! I. Will. Not. Die. Here!" The last note of my shout fell like a falling stone into the muffled silence. The snow was falling thick and fast now and I felt very alone. I glanced down again at Liam and was startled to find his eyes were open and he was staring up at me.

9

Discipline

"Oh gosh, Liam, how d'you feel… okay?" I asked, delighted to see him awake. I wondered if he had heard my strange outburst.

"My head's aching real bad," he groaned, "what happened?"

"A car came round the bend on the wrong side of the road and you had to swerve to avoid it. The truck went over the edge, luckily we didn't roll over. You've been unconscious for a few hours." When he tried to move, I stopped him. "No! You must keep still! Do you hurt anywhere else?"

He thought about that for a moment. "No. Only my head… is it… snowing?"

"Yes," I said, nodding.

Despite my protests, Liam pulled himself up to a sitting position. He looked around. "Where's Jules? Damn… she's not dead?"

"No, no, she's gone to Jim's to fetch help," I reassured him.

"What's the time?" he asked.

I looked at my watch, "Five twenty-five."

"What time did she leave?"

"About three o'clock, I should think. She will be back very soon." I hoped that I sounded convincing.

"We have to find shelter, this snow could be bad. The weather forecast said the fall would be heavy later tonight."

I stared at him and my blood ran cold. "You knew it was going to snow but you still bought us up here?"

"It wasn't supposed to snow until much later on. I figured we had time to get there and back before it started."

Could I trust him? Surely any sane person knowing that bad weather was on the way, would cancel their plans to travel unless it was urgent? It seemed that here in America, people dealt with bad weather more optimistically than in England. There, even the threat of a little snow seemed to paralyse the country.

"Help me up, Claire." Liam tried to stand. I shook my head.

"I don't think we should move from here," I said firmly. "Jules said to stay put and that you shouldn't move."

Liam looked at me and sighed. "Listen, if she left here at three she might not have even arrived at Jim's yet. Another two hours of this snow and we could be as good as dead. Now be a good girl and help me up." I dithered, still not trusting him.

"Claire!" he snapped, "come on now, do as I ask!"

I scrabbled up and hastily scrambled away from him. He looked most surprised and then gave me a lopsided grin. "I didn't realise I was such an ogre!"

I looked uneasily at him. He shook his head at me and then threw off the blankets. Slowly and unsteadily he climbed to his feet. He swayed alarmingly and I hurried to his side to steady him, putting my fears aside. "Thank you," he muttered. He placed an arm over my shoulder and leant on me. We stood that way for a couple of moments, allowing him to adjust to being upright. "Okay so here's the deal, there's a fire hut somewhere north of here as I recall… we should make for that and shelter there overnight."

"Liam, I really think we should stay right here, Jules might not find us otherwise."

"Think, girl. The weather could delay any rescue until tomorrow, by then we could be dead. No, Claire, we need to find shelter and now. Have you a pen and paper in your bag?"

I understood straight away. "We can leave a note!" I exclaimed happily.

"Quite right," he nodded and I grinned back. "Well?" he asked, as I continued to stand grinning at him like a dolt.

"Oh, oh yes, let me look," I said, feeling foolish. I fumbled about amongst the detritus in my bag; I found my, or rather Claire's, address book and a pen. I tore out a page and leaning on the truck, I wrote the note in capital letters: 'JULES WE HAVE GONE TO A FIRE HUT FOR SHELTER. LIAM IS AWAKE. HE SAYS IT IS NORTH OF HERE. LOVE 'N.'—oh, *stupid.* I scribbled out the 'N' hastily and wrote 'CLAIRE.' I glanced over to Liam and realised he had read the note as I wrote it. He didn't seem to notice the oddness of the scribbled out 'N'. He pointed to a large stone, I picked it up and placed the note on the front seat of the truck with the stone on top to anchor it. Then in case it was overlooked, I took out a red lipstick from my bag and drew a large cross on the side window, which had miraculously survived the crash.

Liam nodded approvingly. "Good idea, now fold the tarp and blankets, we'll need 'em." I did as he bid and also took the bag with the coffee and rolls.

When we were ready, Liam turned and walked slowly north past the pickup. I followed on behind, burdened with the heavy tarpaulin and the two blankets which kept slipping down my arms. The snow fell thickly and had begun to cover the ground white. The muffled silence engulfed me and made the situation we were in seem somehow surreal. We plodded onwards for about half an hour. The swirling snow danced dizzily in front of my eyes and made the going difficult and it was impossible to see very far ahead.

Liam stopped and looked around, "I think we turn away from the track about now and head down away into the trees."

I shifted my feet uneasily. "Is that wise?" I asked, remembering my earlier fears. Liam ignored me and began to trudge down toward the trees. I hung back but he soon realised I wasn't with him and turned around looking for me.

"Come on," he called, his voice sounded oddly flat and muffled by the falling snow. I stood and stared at him, uncertain. He muttered softly to himself and trudged back up to me; I stood still waiting for him. He stopped in front of me and studied my face. I looked down at my feet. "What is it?" he asked patiently. I didn't know what to say. I mean I couldn't just ask him straight up, 'Are you going to kill me' now could I? He reached out both hands and I flinched. He grasped my shoulders firmly. "What is it that you are so afraid of, Claire?"

I didn't reply.

"Okay, look I'm not about to hurt you, although if I were feeling a bit stronger I might be tempted to fling you over my shoulder and carry you. I can't understand why you're being so stubborn." My eyes flew up to his, startled. "Don't you worry, I'm too weak to carry you right now." He gave me a half smile.

"Yeah, very funny, big man. For your information I am just wary in case we both end up bloody lost out here!" I hissed crossly.

Liam chuckled. "Wow, temper, temper, little one."

"Shut the hell up, will you!"

"I call that strike two," Liam said calmly. I pulled away from him and stomped off down in the direction he'd indicated towards the trees. My heart beat a fast tattoo and I wondered if he had meant what he said about carrying me. Who did he think he was anyway, Tarzan? I sneered. I wasn't looking where I was going and tripped over a prominent tree root, landing flat on my face in the freezing cold snow. The tarpaulin and blankets broke my fall and it was only my pride that was damaged. Liam held out his hand to help me up, a big grin plastered across his face. Childishly I slapped his hand away and got up on my own, glaring at him.

"Best not forget that I'm trained to deal with little brats like you!" He grinned and winked cheerfully, walking on ahead of me. I tossed my hair out of my eyes and gathered up the load, trudging after him furiously. It was almost dark and I was beginning to think that we were well and truly lost, when Liam gave a shout and waved his arm, pointing ahead into the darkness. I looked and could just make out the angular shape of a small building through the snow. It was the size of a large sized garden shed. Once inside it still struck me as being really cold and it was very dark. Liam went in first and I stood peering in through the doorway. He rummaged about and then a small light appeared; he had lit a candle. "Come on in, darlin'." He flung his arm in an arc of welcome; I didn't hesitate, I was beyond cold. Inside I took a quick look around; I could see the hut was made of wood with a metal corrugated roof. There was a single metal bed with a grubby mattress against one wall. Two chairs stood at the end of the hut, one of them only had three legs. A small black wood-burning stove was set into the wall opposite the bed. There was a sink and a single tap at the top end opposite the door. I went to the bed and put the tarpaulin over the mattress and the blankets on top. That done I turned to look at Liam. He was as white as a sheet and I realised he was completely done in, all bravado gone. I helped him to the bed and after he lay down, I covered him with the blankets. He thanked me and closed his eyes saying, "Get the stove going if you can. There should be kindling outside, someplace out back." Outside, large flakes of snow were falling fast and already carpeting the frozen ground. I found wood stacked up behind the back of the cabin and fetched in three loads, packing the stove tightly. There was a cupboard under the sink and I looked inside hoping to find some matches. I found a saucepan, a frying pan, two mugs, oddly only one plate but no matches.

There was an old bottle of nasty looking dark green stuff, which on closer inspection, turned out to be washing-up-liquid. There was also an extremely ancient box of tea.

I suddenly remembered that Liam had lit a candle when we arrived, so he must have matches on him. He appeared to have fallen asleep and I watched him for a few moments to be sure he was breathing slowly and deeply. I went over to the bed and lifted the blankets. Carefully I slid my hand over his hip pocket, the one nearest to me. No matches there. I stretched down and across him to his other side and bingo, matches. Slowly I tried to slide my hand into his pocket. A hand clamped across my wrist and I gave a startled squeal.

"What are you up to?" Liam growled.

"Matches," I squeaked. He let me go, put his hand into his pocket and wriggled around a bit before handing me a book of matches.

"You only had to ask," he said.

"I thought you were asleep," I told him crossly.

"I was," he said, closing his eyes again. I let out my breath and turned my attention to the fire. Now as you know, in a movie it only takes a second for the hero or heroine to light a fire. Within seconds they have bright flames roaring away. Well, let me tell you, in reality it is *not* so easy. I spent nearly an hour trying to light the damn fire, putting wood in, taking wood out again, then re-adding to it. I trudged in and out fetching little bits of dry bark from the pile outside and scrunching up a few old dry leaves but all to no avail. Then, just as I was about to give up, because, *no* it would *not* catch light, Liam woke up. He got up and lit it and wouldn't you just know it, the damn thing started to burn brightly. I sulked; Liam laughed.

We boiled water and added it to the coffee in the flask. It was weak but not bad, at least it was hot. We ate the rolls too and finished up sharing a bar of chocolate. Then I went outside, to do what a girl's gotta do. Liam made the trip on my return. I was sitting primly on a chair in front of the stove when he got back. "Time for bed, Claire," he said.

I blushed to the roots of my hair. "Umm no, that's okay, you take the bed, I'm fine right here," I told him brightly.

I heard a deep sigh behind me but I wasn't prepared to be scooped up and carried to the bed. I started to squeal and gabble excuses but he growled, "Be quiet, woman and don't be so damn stupid, you can't sit there all night, you'll freeze." He laid me on the bed and sat down, trapping me next to the wall. "Don't worry, I promise not to molest you, never yet had to force a woman to bed with me y'know." He flashed me a grin, then frowned and looked serious. "Hey, you really are scared... I swear I won't hurt you, Claire. I'm a traditional sort of fella when it comes to protecting a woman and I admit that I might *spank* one but I'd never harm one, believe me."

No! I thought. But "Yes," is I what I said.

"Liar," he smiled and his eyes glinted with the colour and warmth of good rye whiskey. "Then, budge over, lady!" He folded himself down next to me and drew me to him, pulling the blankets over us both. I was tense. After a few embarrassing moments he cleared his throat. "Look, hon', I don't know precisely what is going on but I know *something* is not right with you since your accident but I just want to say that you can count on me, Claire, all right?" I didn't reply. I didn't know what on earth to say. "Claire...or whatever your name is."

I stiffened, "What?" I hissed sharply with shock. *Oh my god he knew!*

"Nothin', go to sleep, kitten, you're safe with me." I swear he kissed my hair. I lay awake a long time listening to Liam's even breathing. I knew when he awoke because the deep repetitive breaths changed, they were lighter.

"Liam?" I whispered.

"Mmm?" He was awake.

"How did you come to work for my father?" I asked.

"My folks had a spread, as I told you, in Wyoming. They knew your pa way, way back. When my pa died…"

I sucked in my breath. "I'm sorry."

"Yeah well, it happens. He had a stroke, died three months later. My mom tried to run things for a while; I was… not much help. Anyways, she sold the place eventually. She moved to her sister's in Denver." He fell silent.

"Did you visit us at all, I don't recall?' I was worried, I should know and hoped my 'accident' would cover any blunders I made here.

"Nah, my mom met your pa by accident a few years ago. She filled him in with our sad tale and he offered me a job. I jumped at the chance of working on a ranch, being around horses again. Using my psychology to help troubled girls and the odd boy, it was the icing on the cake for me an' I took the opportunity on offer. I owe your pa a lot you know."

"Don't you, um, find doling out discipline to the kids an awkward thing to do?" I rushed on, my face burning, "I mean don't the parents complain?"

Liam cocked his head to one side, his eyes narrowed thoughtfully. "Hmm, well, most of the time I interview the kids and their folks before they come to the ranch. I go visit them in their own homes and discuss the kid's conduct to date and the parent's expectations for their child's behaviour in the future—you'd be surprised how many parents see normal teenage behaviour as abnormal. The whole family is talked through the discipline package before they sign a consent form. Then I decide if I want to take the kid, based on whether I think they can be rehabilitated or not. When a teen leaves the ranch after six weeks, they are presented with a paddle that they have helped to carve a chosen homily on. They get to take it home with them. In my follow up call to the parents, usually three weeks after the teen leaves us, I occasionally find parents have used the paddles to straighten their kids out back home. You know, in my experience, there are no 'bad' kids, just damaged kids and sick kids but mostly it's just a case of bad parenting. No boundaries set or too high an expectation perhaps with learning at school, y'know?"

I bristled. "Hey, but that's not fair. In that case, you could blame Mr. and Mrs. Hitler for what their son did to Europe!"

Liam chuckled. "Well now, y'all know they say the worst mistake in recent years was when Mr. Hitler suggested an early night to his Mrs. on the night of Adolf's conception!"

Laughing despite myself, I shoved him with my elbow. "That's a *terrible* joke; don't let me hear you tell it again!"

"Do you think we should hire more trained staff to help take on more kids? There seems to be a lot of dysfunctional families out there and I can see this becoming a much needed support," Liam asked.

"What is the highest number at any one time that you feel comfortable dealing with?"

"Well, after my experience with young Kate, I prefer a one-to-one approach."

Kate at the ranch...? I was caught off guard. "Remind me," I said, warily.

"Oh yeah, you were still at college back then, you probably don't remember what an ornery critter little Kate was when she first came to us. We had three girls that summer and Kate was the worst of all three. She lived with her grandparents—she'd lost both her parents. Her father died of a work related accident in a steel works and then her mother died from cancer a few years later, a rough deal for a small girl. Kate needed one-to-one care but I was spread too thin. She was the only one of the three girls that summer who got paddled on a regular basis. She took off once on Sasha, surely you remember that?"

"Mm—hmm." I nodded an affirmative.

"Anyway, all 'water under the bridge' now. I mean look how well Kate turned out! She's just great at helping me out in the bunkhouse with those 'terrible teens', she's turned her whole life around, a real success story!"

Hmm, I was not so sure, food for thought.

I decided to change the subject. "What about your photography?" I was so intrigued by those fabulous photographs.

"That was a college course I didn't finish. I guess I was too young to know what a jerk I was dumping photography… but you know I have never regretted it. I love my work.

I'll just bet you do—spanking all those naughty bottoms! Stop it—Stop it right now! What the hell was wrong with me?

"I love photography too. I can even process my own prints, I…" I stopped, flustered. Foolishly, I had been about to tell him about my dark room, my love of film and media. I had forgotten that Claire had no such passion.

"I didn't know you could process. You're good with a camera though, those shots you took at your pa's party last year were real good."

I breathed a sigh of relief; my sister and I were more alike under the skin than I had guessed. "Thank you," I said softly.

"Can I ask you something personal?" Liam asked.

"Sure." I wondered what was coming.

"Are you and Matt serious?"

"Noo… I don't think so," I answered, cautiously.

"Well, has he asked you to marry him?"

"Kind-a."

"Well, I call that serious, missy."

"Gee whizz, well maybe he is, but I'm *not!*"

"Seems to me you should tell the poor guy that and not string him along."

"Oh I'm sure he knows." I was getting uncomfortable with this line of questioning.

Liam gave me a stern look. "You sure about that?"

"Yes. Why are you so interested?" I asked, nettled.

"No reason. Claire?"

"Yes?"

"Do you think we could possibly go to sleep now?"

"Cheek… hey you were the one asking all the questions! *Good night!*" I turned over with a huff.

"Bratty girl, you and I both know darned well that I'm gonna end up spanking you one of these days—jus' a friendly warning." I stiffened but refrained from answering and heard him give a rumbling chuckle. I smiled and closed my heavy lids, immediately drifting off to sleep.

When I woke, it was daylight. I was lying across his chest. His arm was flung over my hip. I lay very still, listening to the rise and fall of his even breathing beneath my cheek. He smelt good. Liam was male, musky and warm. Amazingly, I felt safe for the first time since I arrived in Arizona. Carefully so as not to wake him, I lifted my head to look at his face, his eyes were shut. The lashes lay thick and dark but a large bluish bruise had appeared along his forehead. He had a shadow of stubble over his lower jaw. He had a strong jaw and a rugged face. Gently, unthinkingly I placed my lips to the dark bruise. I drew back quickly, wondering what on earth I was doing. My heart jumped in shock as Liam's eyes opened, gazing at me, his expression unreadable. "Good morning to you too," he said gruffly.

"Umm, you have a nasty bruise on your head. My mother always said, 'Feed a cold, starve a fever, and er....*kiss a bruise*'!" I improvised and gabbled quickly, adding to that well known homily as I was disconcerted at being caught kissing him.

"Hey, is it still snowing?" rumbled Liam.

"Shall I take a look?" Gratefully, I grasped the chance to escape my stupid blunder. I clambered over him and went to the door. It was difficult to open; the snow had piled up high against the outside of the cabin. It was still snowing but not as heavily. Outside it was a changed world, a white wonderland. "It's easing up a bit," I called. "Oooh do come see—it's so beautiful out here." I felt Liam's presence move up behind me. He put his hands on my shoulders. I leaned back against him and we gazed in silence at the sparkling radiance that surrounded us.

He broke the spell first. "I wish I had my camera," he sighed.

"I know. I wish I had one too, even my sketch pad would do; it all looks so amazing."

"Mmm, kinda pure and totally untouched." He took a deep breath of the cold clean air and turned to me. "Okay, how about a hot drink? Warm us both up a bit."

"We finished the last of the coffee last night," I told him.

"There's tea," he said turning back inside the hut. I followed him in and dug out my boots from underneath the bed. I sat on the side of the bed and pulled them on, while Liam fed wood into the stove, blowing gently on the embers until a flame flickered into life.

"How do you feel today?" I asked him.

"Yeah, I'm good," he replied with a nod. He closed the stove door and turned to the cupboard under the sink. He pulled out the very, very old crumpled box of tea.

"Is that tea okay to drink, d'you reckon?" I asked, looking at it doubtfully.

He sniffed at the contents of the box. "Smells good to me but then I don't drink tea in the normal way of things."

I reached over and turned on the tap but nothing happened. "Blast, no water. The pipes must be frozen." Picking up the old saucepan we had used the night before, Liam headed for the door. "Where are you going?" I asked him anxiously.

"Snow." He threw the word over his shoulder and was gone. I shrugged and reached for my handbag. I brushed my hair back and applied some of Claire's pale lipstick. Liam came back in with a pan full of snow, which he placed on top of the stove to heat.

"Clever," I said, nodding approvingly. I could feel a call of nature coming on and went to the door.

"Where do you think you're going?" Liam asked.

"Snow," I replied, mimicking him and looking back over my shoulder with a grin.

"Yeah, very funny," he called after me. I giggled and pulled the door shut behind me.

We ate the last of the food Jules had packed into the rucksack—two apples. At least the tea was hot and afterwards I rinsed the pan and mugs out with boiled snow. "Shall we walk back to the pickup now?" I asked as I worked.

Liam was folding the blankets. "If the snow stops, then sure," he replied.

"Well it has stopped, hasn't it?" I asked.

"Not totally, no."

"But it's only light flurries, I think we should go," I said determined to leave.

"No, Claire, it may come down heavily all of a sudden, we could get lost. At least here we are warm and dry." He was adamant.

I banged the pan down on the cupboard shelf. "I have no intention of spending another night here alone with you. Besides, the food's all gone and we need to eat soon! I intend to walk back to the truck. You do what you want."

Liam stilled, gazing at me steadily and silently. It was unnerving and I could feel his eyes boring into me. "What?" I asked crossly. He continued to gaze at me and I noticed a faint tick in his jaw. "What the *hell's* wrong with you now?" I demanded, tetchily.

"You," he replied at last.

"What d'you mean, '*you*'?" He was really getting to me y'know—how did he do it? One minute we were getting along just fine and the next I wanted to slap him.

He shook his head, turned his back on me heading for the door.

"Pig," I muttered, loud enough for him to hear. He paused in the process of opening the door, carefully closed it again and turned around real slow. I stepped back, alarmed by the implacable look on his face. He walked over to me and stood almost touching me, invading my personal space. I gulped and fixed my eyes on his chest.

"That's the third strike," he said tersely. How did he change his voice like that? I didn't know what he meant but it sounded *very* bad. He continued to stand there saying nothing.

My stomach lurched and I shuffled nervously, the silence was so uncomfortable that I just had to speak, but when I did, my voice didn't sound anything like me. "What d'you mean?" I squeaked in a falsetto voice.

"I think you know that baseball term, Claire, and you certainly know the rules."

No, no I didn't know… to both those statements! Liam lifted his hand to my chin and tilted my face up so he could look down into my eyes. I noticed that his cinnamon irises, had flecks of gold within them and that his lashes were a dark coffee colour and not black as I had first thought.

"You, young lady, are going over my knee for a well-deserved spanking."

I could barely comprehend his words. Shock and embarrassment were my first reaction, my second was flight. I had barely begun to tense my knees, rising to the balls of my feet, when I was swung upwards and sideways, landing squarely over Liam's knee in a smooth and expertly executed action by Mr. Disciplinarian himself. I found myself face down on the bed, my head on my arms in the blankets and my jean clad behind positioned up in the air over his hard thigh. I tried to push up and off the bed but Liam clamped his arm over my waist and at the same time, one of his legs scooted up and over mine. I was trapped. Damn, the man was quick!

With no warning at all. a hard *thwup* landed on my seat, rapidly followed by another. My brain was trying to cope with so many different emotions that I was overwhelmed and flopped still where I was pinned. I was receiving my *first* ever spanking, something I had thought about, dreamed about, *fantasized* about for goodness sake—and for years. Yet I was shocked and unprepared —it hurt! *Should it hurt?* Surely it should feel *sexy* but instead it was —deeply embarrassing. I was so immersed in my own confused thoughts that it took me awhile to realise that Liam was talking to me.

".....and so, actions have consequences, young lady, and this is the consequence of your rude and brattish behaviour. I gave you fair warning, giving you the usual three strikes. I even told you that you were being a brat but you chose to ignore me." I was squirming now because despite the fact my behind was denim clad, the continued, fast delivered and surprisingly hard, swats were setting my rear end alight. I couldn't help but moan. "Good, I'm getting through to you, am I? Well, Claire, you may be the boss's daughter, darlin', and you may have had an injury but that does *not* give you the right to disrespect other folk and bad mouth them whenever you feel like it!" This lecture was punctuated with some jaw breaking *thwacks* to my tender posterior and to my chagrin, I began to plead with him to stop.

"I'll stop when I think you are a truly sorry, little girl and not just uncomfortable from being spanked," he told me smugly. I ground my teeth and hissed a bad cuss word at him. I don't know if he heard me or not, but he speeded up the swats with gusto and I decided that I'd had more than enough, *thank you very much*!

I bit his leg.

This was a *mistake.*

Note to future self:

When being spanked, do not bite!

Out of embarrassment, I hesitate to write this part down. I think I will for now but perhaps I'll remove it at a later date.

Liam very deftly divested me of my panties and jeans. The man is a *demon.* At this point I think that I hated him—and John Wayne, who had made me think that I might actually *enjoy* this whole spanking lark. I thought that I was embarrassed before but now… I was *mortified*!

And sore! My brain was receiving severe burn messages from my scalding rump. I had no other thought in my head other than, *'My bottom is scorching—somebody, help me—Please!'*

What I actually yelped out was, "I am sooo sor-ry, I am sooo sor-ry, please, Liam I am sooo sor-ry!" Over and over again I chanted my mantra, in the desperate hope that he would finally stop spanking me.

I don't know if he got bored of hearing my pleas, or perhaps his arm was dropping off, but finally he stopped chastising me. He rested his hand on my throbbing derriere and allowed me to catch my breath. He asked me what I had to say to him. I took a deep breath and apologized as sincerely as I could.

"Okay, Claire, I think you may have learned a lesson here today."

Actually I have learned that I do not wish to be spanked ever again, thank you!

I certainly wasn't going to tell Liam that and so I mumbled an agreement and stood up on shaky legs. Liam pulled up my panties and jeans. I was standing between his thighs and I just couldn't look him in the face. I was startled when he pulled me forward into his arms for a hug. I held myself stiffly but he put a hand on the back of my head and pushed my head onto his shoulder. "There now, Claire, it's all over an' forgotten," he said gruffly. For some strange reason his gentleness set me off and I found myself flooded with tears and burying my nose into his neck—weird huh? The other strange thing was he smelled so good, so fresh and male that I didn't want to move. I burrowed in and Liam eased me onto his lap and cradled me as I cried. After a while, he lifted out a large handkerchief and told me to blow. I did and then he dried my eyes. "You needed that didn't you, little one? I suspect it's eased the tension that has been building up inside you ever since the incident at Pinto Rock. I knew when you were so waspish and rude the other day that this was coming."

I snapped my head up in surprise. "You mean you thought that I needed to be umm...*spanked*?"

Liam nodded and gave me a self-assured grin. "I am *very* good at my job you know."

"Yeah, I just found that out!" I said reaching under my behind to give it a tentative pat. "Ouch!"

Liam laughed. "No—I mean I'm a good behavioural psychologist—I *know* I'm a darn good spanker!" I flushed red and he chuckled again. I couldn't help it, I laughed with him. In fact, I became slightly hysterical, probably from embarrassment, and I began to howl with mirth, until I had tears rolling down my cheeks and you know what? Liam joined in. Yeah, we clutched each other and rolled around on that bed with aching stomachs and we guffawed. Finally, I rolled to the edge of the bed and sat on the side, wiping my eyes. He was right, I felt so much better, less tense and very much alive. I was raring to go.

THE SNOW HAD STOPPED FALLING, the skies were blue again and the sun was shining. The brilliance caught at tiny crystals of snow and turned them into sparkling silver. Soft muffled thumping sounds were all around me and I wondered what the noise could be. The fir trees looked like tall brides, their tiered branches dressed in layers of silvery white. As I gazed, I saw a laden fir tree drop an avalanche of powdery snow to the ground below which solved the strange thumping noise. Flurries of snow drifted down from the higher branches like white confetti. A dark shape to the left caught my eye and I saw Liam come out of the small cabin laden with the blankets and tarp. I waved and he grinned, calling out, "We should start walking back up to the pickup!" I nodded and hastened over to divest him of the blankets.

The walk back was much easier than the day before, despite the fact it was hard going in the deep virgin snow. Unburdened by the heavy tarp helped; Liam carried it and I held the blankets, I wore one and carried the other. Unlike the day before, it was sunny and clear. The snow was a foot or more deep in places, which made our progress slow. I enjoyed it; I loved the crunch of snow under my feet and the clean white of the landscape surrounding us. Blue shadows in the dips and dells, reflections from icicles twinkling from branches on deciduous trees. When we arrived back at the accident site, we found the damaged truck covered in a thick layer of snow. "No one has been to look for us yet," Liam said.

"How do you know?" I asked.

"No footprints," he said with a shrug.

I bent down, gathered a handful of snow, and shaped it before throwing it at the back of his neck. "Know all!" I shrieked gleefully, as my aim struck true.

Liam spun around surprised. "Hey, girl...just you wait!" he yelled, gathering snow himself and staggering through the drifts toward me. I turned and fled stumbling through the deep powdery mounds, laughing all the while. I felt a scattering thump on my back and bent to scoop up more ammunition to throw back in return. Once again my aim was true and I crowed with glee. Liam's face was determined as he ran towards me. I shrieked again and turned to run. Before I knew what had hit me, he dove and we rolled around on the ground, pillowed together in the loose snow. He straddled my waist as I lay on my back laughing up at him. Then his face changed, his smile went and my heart raced at the intense expression in his bright, clear eyes. He lowered his head and I knew that he would kiss me. Then a deep thrumming noise filtered through my foggy brain, a repetitive drone, a helicopter! Liam shaded his eyes against the glare and, straightening up, he waved. Jules, a woman of many talents apparently, was in the cockpit and she gave us a thumbs-up sign as a medic leapt down from the helicopter. We were rescued.

10

Confusion

I didn't see Liam for a while after our dramatic rescue, not until the day before the party. We had been flown to the nearest hospital, which was luckily at Flagstaff, by the Huey rescue helicopter and given a complete health check. Liam was treated for a minor concussion and bruising. My anxious father awaited us at the hospital and arranged for us to be taken home. Harry, the man with the extra trestle tables we were going to collect, delivered them himself once the roads were clear, on the day before the party. With all the arrangements to be made, there was no time for me to seek Liam out, even if I had wanted to, which actually I didn't. I was disconcerted by my own eager response to that near kiss. The thought of what might have been had the helicopter not arrived when it did, was keeping me awake at night. Well, that and the spanking he had given me!

I did meet with Matt, however, the following morning he came to see if I was recovered from my adventure. He seemed ill at ease and eager to be gone as soon as possible. This won't do, I thought. To the world, we must appear as friendly and at ease as always. I dragged him into the house to talk. "Look here, Matt," I hissed, keeping my voice down, "you've got to behave as you've *always* done when you were around Claire."

"It's real hard for me to do that, Miss."

"Claire!" I corrected him.

"Sorry, see that there's the problem."

"Listen, Matt, we need to talk and we must be seen out and about together. Why don't you take me out for dinner tonight?"

"Dinner… jus' you an' me?" He looked terrified.

"Yes. Where did you take my sister in the evenings?"

"Um, well mainly the Spotted Steer jus' for a couple of beers, there's a real good band mostly."

"That sounds a bit noisy, we need to talk. What about somewhere to eat, a steak house perhaps, my treat?" I smiled at him encouragingly.

"We-ll, there's Mister Macho's, I guess."

"Great, what time?"

"I'll pick you up at seven." Matt turned to leave but stopped suddenly, looking back at me. "If'n we're gonna do this right, the way me an' Claire did, then I pick up the bill. Okay?"

I nodded. "Cool, fine by me."

At seven o'clock as agreed Matt pulled up outside the main door in his truck. I ran around and climbed in the passenger seat. As I closed the vehicle's door, I noticed Liam crossing the yard. He stopped and watched us pull away; his face was expressionless and unreadable. He made no gesture in return to my cheery wave; I felt guilty and caught out and wondered why I should feel this way.

The steak house was a friendly, homely place and quite a few people lifted a hand in greeting toward us when we arrived. Matt led me to a table by the window. The red and white checked tablecloth was freshly laundered and a small vase of fresh flowers stood in the centre of the table. The waitress placed a jug of water and two glasses on the table, handing us our menus before saying, "Hi-ya, Matt, Claire, what can I get y'all to drink right now?"

Matt ordered two Ballantine beers and he spoke quickly, glancing at me, afraid, I think, that I might interrupt him. "Then our usual, Marie, thanks."

"Okay now, so that's two Ballantine's 'n one medium steak 'n one double egg 'n fries, comin' right up!"

Matt looked at me sheepishly, "Sorry, Claire always had eggs, her being vegetarian an all."

"That's fine, Matt. Now talk to me. I can understand that this has been a terrible ordeal for you. You must miss Claire so much!"

Matt nodded but said nothing for a while. I waited, determined not to speak just to fill an awkward silence; my patience was eventually rewarded.

"It just doesn't seem possible that she's gone, y'know? When I see you, I feel real sick inside, no reflection on yourself," he added hastily.

"I understand," I said quietly, "but please talk to me, Matt."

He looked down at the table avoiding eye contact, then began to speak quietly. "I loved her so much. I dunno if she felt the same way 'bout me but she liked me an awful lot, ah know she did." He looked up then and I saw that his eyes shone with unshed tears. "She told me things, we talked, shared stuff y'know?"

I leaned forward. "What sort of things?" I asked eagerly.

"Dunno, jus' 'bout everything I guess," he said, shrugging. He looked so bereft that I covered his hand with my own.

"Matt, did Claire ever mention anything wrong about the dude side of things up at the ranch?"

"How d' you mean… what kinda wrong?"

"I don't really know. Maybe with the books or something like that."

Matt thought for a moment before answering. "Well now, she

was real het up over a few things there, the dude side of things, the casino, arguments with her pa—"

I interrupted, "With our father?"

"Yeah, they was fighting big time up till the day she was killed. I even wondered if 'n he done it for a while back there."

I gasped. "You think my father…"

"Nah, I did wonder, then I realised it was a stupid idea, he adored her."

With a sickening feeling, I remembered my own early suspicions about our father. Could it possibly have been him? Would he have killed his *own daughter* and if so why and why involve me? I rubbed my aching temples. He had suggested that we take a break, a trip away after the party. Was that so he could arrange an accident for me too? But what could my father possibly gain from my death? I was deep in contemplation and jumped when a clatter of plates announced the arrival of the waitress with our food.

"Steak 'n fries for you and eggs for you, can I refresh y'alls drinks? No? Okay, enjoy y'alls meal now!" The waitress placed the dishes before us and we stopped talking for a few minutes while we ate the gargantuan portions of chips, eggs and in Matt's case, the biggest steak I'd ever seen.

Finally I asked, "Who do you suspect then, Matthew?"

His gaze flicked up and met mine, I lowered my gaze to my plate. I knew from that look he suspected someone. "Come on," I wheedled, "we have to catch whoever did this. After all, I could be next." Despite my bravado, I shivered.

"Look." Matt put down his cutlery. "I've got a gut feeling but nothing to go on an' I can't go around making accusations without any proof."

"But, Matt, I'm only asking you to share your thoughts with me. Work together, pool information. I won't tell anyone else what you tell me. We have to trust each other here. Look, if I share what I suspect with you, then I think you should do the same with me, agreed?" He sighed deeply but nodded. I waited and realised when he took a mouthful of beer that he wanted to hear my thoughts first. "Okay, I think Claire stumbled onto some irregularities on the dude side of the ranch and someone," I couldn't bring myself to say Liam, "killed her to protect them from exposure. When I agreed to impersonate Claire like this I was certain at first that no one would try to kill again because it was a case of a one off murder by a nut case. I know now that I was wrong, someone tried to kill Claire again the other night."

Matt slammed down his beer.

"Shit! When, how?" Matt stared at me, horrified.

"In the bath two nights ago. The lights went off and some-one, I think it was a man, well, the bastard tried to drown me in my bath."

"How did you escape?" Matt was totally shocked.

"I hit him over the head with a jar of bath oil."

Matt laughed, shaking his head. "Holy cow, Nicola, you've sure got some spirit, lady!" I smiled thinly; it was all too real for me to find anything about that night amusing.

"So, who'd you think it was?"

"Well, as to that, I'm just not sure," I prevaricated.

"You mean you suspect someone right?"

I sighed, "I don't know, Matt, but I did wonder about Liam. Do you know where he was on the morning that Claire was murdered?"

Matt looked thoughtful. "Hmm, I'm fairly sure he was up on top of the bunkhouses, mending the roof. I saw him up there when I rode out to look for Claire later that morning."

I leaned toward Matt. "Could he possibly have ridden out, killed Claire and climbed back up onto the roof before you left?"

He clicked his tongue. "I was in the tack room, sorting out the order for the next six months, I jus' don't know an' that's the truth." He ran both hands agitatedly through his thick hair. "I've gone over it and over it. Your pa was away overnight, so only the housekeeper and Claire were at the ranch the night before. Liam and I were the only ones around. I didn't kill her so who are we left with?"

I leaned back in my chair and shook my head sadly. I couldn't believe how devastated I felt at the certainty of Liam's guilt.

"I personally think it has to have been Liam O'Donnell," I told Matt flatly. He nodded sadly.

"Yeah, I think so too, but why, I mean what motive can he have? It just don't make no sense… y'know?"

"Could there have been anything going on between the two of them that you didn't know about?" He looked up sharply. "I'm sorry, Matt, but I have to ask you this," I coaxed gently.

He nodded. "I know and I've asked myself the same question a million times. Liam treated Claire like a kid sister. When she finished college she was so full of herself. Thought she knew it all. She and Liam got on up 'til then. They only rubbed up the wrong way when Claire tried to tell him how to run the dude side of things." Matt stopped talking, he looked thoughtful.

"Go on," I pressed.

"Liam told her to stay out of his business in no uncertain terms. Y'know he runs that discipline set-up and likes to spank?" I flushed and nodded, *oh yeah, I certainly knew that!* "Well now, he threatened her an' so I went to see him, an' I told him, darn it, no one spanks my lady but me o' course. Not that ah ever did."

What was it with these cowboys and spanking?

"I bet she was just thrilled," I said sarcastically. Matt seemed to miss my sarcasm completely.

"Yeah well, I never told her that part. Anyhow Claire talked to her pa but he took Liam's side. Claire was furious but she was real hurt too. Carl eventually gave Claire responsibility for the accounts for both the dude ranch and the casino in Vegas. She accepted but chafed at not being in charge of either outfit. I think she felt Carl didn't trust her." Matt fell silent, deep in reverie. I sat quietly, pondering what Matt had just told me.

"Matt, did Claire tell you that she had found irregularities in any of the accounts?" I asked after a while.

"She was excited about something she'd found out about, yeah. I don't know if it was the books or something else."

"So when did she tell you all this?" I asked.

"About a week before her death, she asked me to meet her. She said her daddy would have to put her in charge once he knew what was going on." Matt stopped talking.

"And?" I prompted.

"That's it. She wouldn't tell me anymore, said it was a secret much too important to share. That's when we fell out."

"Tell me, Matt… please."

"I said if we were gonna be married then there must be trust between us. She said she wasn't sure about us and wanted to cool it for a little while, said she needed time to think about her future. I got mad. I'm not real proud of that but I had waited for her, putting my life on hold for two years. She made me promises that now she was breaking… excuse me, call of nature." Abruptly Matt got up and walked away. I watched him weave his way between the dinner tables. He was a strange young man; he obviously found it difficult to talk about his feelings for Claire and I wasn't sure how much he was hiding from me.

I found myself wondering if Matt had been angry enough with Claire to kill her. If so, why would he try to kill me in the bath that night when he already knew Claire was dead and I was an imposter? Unless, the dark thought suddenly struck me, it was a false attempt on my life, a smoke screen to put me off the scent. Matt could have killed Claire and I could be sitting here cosily tonight with my sister's murderer. My head began to throb painfully, I was going around in vicious circles. Just as I thought I had everything worked out in my mind, something else cropped up and the whole hypothesis went awry. Matt returned and I stood up. "Look, if you don't mind, Matt, I'd like to call it a night, I'm really very tired and perhaps we could we just leave now?"

Matt hesitated then reached out and took my hand in his. "I know what you're thinking, that maybe I killed Claire. I swear I didn't, Nicola. I loved her. She was my life. I couldn't have hurt her. She was sweet and funny and beautiful and now she's gone forever." His eyes were brimming with tears and I couldn't bear to see such pain. I reached up impulsively and hugged him.

"I do know," I whispered, "I'm so sorry, Matt, what do you plan to do now that she's gone?"

Matt shrugged his shoulders. "I got draft papers for 'Nam a while back and I'm off soon as the police give the go-ahead." I was sad to think that Matt's future was a faraway war, it seemed so bleak a future for Claire's fiancée, he deserved better.

"Hey y'all two love birds, d'ya want dessert?" We moved apart and shook our heads at the waitress.

"No thanks, hon', can I have the check please?" Matt asked her.

No more was said and we hardly spoke on the journey home. He dropped me at the house and agreed to partner me for the dance on Saturday night.

11

Menace

Friday and Saturday were a hive of activity. Men were everywhere, putting up a temporary dance floor with a canopy above, setting up trestle tables, hanging lights all around the outside of the barn and house. Baskets of flowers arrived and I was put to work by Sarah, making long garlands with the sweet smelling greenery. I had to twine together the flowers with yards of green and orange Mexican coloured ribbon. These were then draped around the canopy of the dance area. More flowers in hot tropical colours were to stand in huge vases in all the corners. Smaller versions sat on top of the bright orange and green chequered tablecloths. The small covered tables were arranged in the area below the dance platform, forming a bright outer circle. Chinese paper lanterns were strung above the tables and from the barn and house roof. The overall scene looked rather wonderful, magical and quite unlike any party decor that I had seen before. I was filled with anticipation, especially since the weather now favoured us with some luke-warm sunshine.

Food was brought out in bulk from the enormous walk in freezer to defrost overnight. I helped to carry frozen steaks and piles of Sarah's homemade meat loaf into the kitchen. The freezer was almost cleared out when I went back for the last remaining steaks. I was at the back of the small icy room when the door swung shut and I was suddenly engulfed in solid darkness. At first I remained calm and felt my way to the door. I banged on the thick steel and yelled. "Hello, I'm in here… hey, let me out, is anyone out there?" I listened, I could hear absolutely nothing. I felt panic rise as I began to shiver from the icy cold within the freezer. Then I recalled my walkie-talkie and pulled it out with difficulty from inside my pocket. My fingers were getting progressively numb with cold so it was hard to hold the small hand set. I pressed the transmit button but, as I did so, I wondered feverishly whether Jules would be able to receive a signal from within the thick walls of the glacial room. I kept pressing the talk button and repeating 'over' into the hand set but there was no response.

I banged, kicked and thumped as loudly as I could on the chilled metal door and I called out until I was hoarse. I decided that I must try to keep warm, so I began to jump up and down. My teeth were chattering uncontrollably and I was shivering in the invasive arctic air. Time crawled, the blackness was absolute. I tried so hard to keep moving but I ended up leaning up against the freezing metal wall, my bones were stiff with the cold that had worked its way deep inside my cringing flesh. I cried briefly but I lost energy even for that basic emotion so relentless was the penetrating frost around me. I began to feel sleepy and I suppose I must have slept briefly for I have no recollection of the freezer door opening. The first thing I recall is Liam's face looking thunderous as he studied my face and bawled for some help. He scooped me up, one arm under my shoulders another under my knees. I tried to talk but my teeth chattered so violently it was difficult to speak. Liam bent his head to mine and shushed me gently, "Hush now, sweetheart, you don't need to worry, I'm here now."

I struggled to speak. "Ttt… th… th… the door sw… shwung… h… sh… Shu… o… o… on mm… mm… me," I managed to stutter. Sarah and Kate arrived with blankets and Matt rushed up, his face strained and white.

Liam nodded to him. "I'm going to carry her inside, Matt. You go on ahead and build the biggest fire that you can. Sarah, you go make a bed on the sofa with blankets and a hot water bottle, we must get her warm—Kate go run a hot bath. Okay, stand back everyone." Liam adjusted me in his arms and when he turned, I saw that quite a crowd had gathered. I turned my befuddled face into his shoulder, embarrassed by all the strange faces staring at me. Liam shouldered his way through the throng and carried me through the kitchen door and into the house. In the main living room, Matt was kneeling at the fire place with a good blaze building before him. Sarah had cleared the sofa and placed pillows and blankets ready at one end. Liam lowered me gently onto the makeshift bed and tucked the blankets around me. Kate produced hot water bottles for my feet and then ran off to fill a bath, followed by Sarah. Liam whipped off my shoes and begun to rub my chilled feet between his hands.

Everyone started to speak at once, so I shut my eyes and lay back, clenching my teeth against their continuous chattering. My feet started to ache. "Ow… g… g… gently!" My eyes flew open and I tried to pull my feet away from Liam's grasp but he gripped me firmly and continued his fierce rubbing.

"Good, you're getting some feeling back into them." I lifted my head and glowered at him down the length of my body.

Before I could say anything else, a bellow from the doorway interrupted. "Nicola, what the hell's happened?" My father burst into the room and stumbled to my side. He knelt and took me in his arms rather awkwardly.

"I'm f… f… f… fine," I managed to say, still trying to control my chattering teeth. Then I hissed into his ear. "C… C… Claire!"

He hunkered back on his heels and looked down at me, nodding to show he understood. "Claire, what happened?" It seemed that his question was an invitation for everyone to jump in and speak at once. My father stood up. "Right, that's it, everyone out!" Most people turned and left the room at once, others lingered, staring at me until my father shooed them all out. An audible muttering could be heard, even as my father closed the doors behind them. I only realised that Liam had stayed behind in the room with us when he threw back the covers and begun massaging my calves vigorously. I jerked my leg out of his hand at the pain but he firmly pulled it back and when I kicked out at him, he gave my calf a sharp smack. I jerked my head up off the pillows and gave him a furious glare; he had the audacity to wink. Before I could scold him, my father claimed my attention, asking again what had happened to me. I explained as best I could and he looked sombre as he listened. "By design there is no way that door could have swung shut on its own," he said.

"W… w… why?" I asked."

"It's sprung, designed to stay open until actually pushed closed, a safety mechanism because it's a walk-in freezer. This was a deliberate act of mischief."

"Yup, I agree," said Liam nodding; my father seemed to notice him for the first time.

"Did you see anything or anyone, O'Donnell?" he asked, sounding abrupt.

"Nope, I was keeping an eye on Claire and when she disappeared for a while, I asked around to see if anyone had seen her. Sarah said she was helping carry from the freezer so I decided to check inside and—bingo."

"Thank you for keeping her safe, Liam," my father said fervently. "I've lost one special gift and I won't lose another!"

"Dad," I protested weakly, but he seemed oblivious to his faux-pas. Liam was silent and when I stole a peek at him he was engrossed in chaffing the skin from my poor legs. Perhaps he hadn't understood what my father had meant. The door opened and Jules came into the room.

"Okay, no need to explain, I know what's happened," she said before anyone could speak.

"It most certainly is not okay!" my father growled, "where the hell were you, young woman? I expected you to look after my daughter and someone has tried to kill her twice now and on both occasions you are nowhere to be seen!"

Jules glanced meaningfully at Liam. "I think you should just pipe down, Mr. Keedon! Liam, can you carry Claire upstairs; I have seen Sarah and she told me to tell you that a hot bath is all ready and waiting for our frozen chicken."

Father was beet red but he took a deep breath and turned to Liam. "D'you mind carrying her, son? Can you manage my girl all on your own?"

Liam stood up and stretched. "Yeah, sure thing, no problem, Carl." He came around to the side of the settee and before I could protest, he had me all scooped up blankets and all. He then proceeded to carry me out into the hallway. People crowded around fussing, it seemed the hall was full. I tightened my arms around Liam's neck and buried my head into his shoulder again, unable to cope with their questions and kindly curiosity. Liam dealt with them firmly and sent them all back to their tasks, continuing on up the stairs with me held gently in his arms. I marvelled at his strength and the feel of his smooth hard muscles under my hands. I told him so too. He winked again and his mouth quirked upwards in a sinful grin. My heart beat jarringly and I found myself thinking how much I liked the way his eyes crinkled up at the corners when he smiled at me like that.

"You're no weight at all, Nicola," he told me and I could see he was watching me intently, waiting to see how I would react to the name.

I thought fast. "How did you know I was called Nicola-Claire?"

"I didn't," he replied, "your father called you that downstairs and after the truck accident you said something about being called Nicola."

"Ah, well I was christened Nicola Claire Keedon but I *hate* the name Nicola. So everyone calls me by my second name, Claire, d'you see?" My heart was hammering at the lie and I hoped he couldn't feel it against his ribs.

"I see, so your real name *is* Nicola?"

"I guess." I tried to sound casual and unconcerned.

"Nice name, don't see why you would dislike it." He looked at me intently, inclining his head and smiling slightly. I think he believed me and I felt myself go limp with relief.

We arrived at my bedroom and Kate was there, waiting to help me, so Liam deposited me on the bed and left me in her capable hands. He gave me an awkward pat on my shoulder and told me, "Try and stay out of trouble, brat," before returning to the hubbub below. I had a long soak in the bath and a short while later Jules came up and sat on the bed to talk to me through the open bathroom door. The heat from the bath water felt heavenly and I slid down so that my chin rested on top of the water and I sighed with contented bliss at being warm again.

"What do you remember before you went into the freezer?" she asked me.

"Nothing helpful at all," I told her.

"Come on, Claire, who was near you? Close your eyes and think."

I did as she asked but nothing unusual came to mind. "No good," I told her, 'I can't recall anyone or anything odd at all."

Jules was so silent that I wondered if she had left the bedroom. "Hello, Jules?" I called out worriedly.

"Yeah?"

"I thought you'd left, you went quiet on me."

"No, I'm thinking about things. Look, Claire, as soon as the party is over, I do want you and your father to go away for that vacation break, as he suggested. Things are happening here too fast and I want time to go see my boss and look into a few discrepancies."

"What kind of discrepancies?" I asked puzzled.

"Doesn't matter…"

"Oh yes it does, this is my life that's at stake here!" I was incensed.

"Can I come in there?" she asked.

"Yeah okay," I replied. She entered the bathroom and hunkered down beside the bathtub to study my face.

"Look, Claire, this person is very dangerous and very clever. There's something else going on here and I can't make it out yet. Until I do, you will be safer away from here, just for a while."

I nodded and decided to fill her in on my recent conversation with Matt.

"You seriously suspect Liam then?" she asked, seeming surprised.

"Well, yes, don't you?"

"Not really, no, but now you've sown me a seed of doubt." She looked even more worried.

"Well, who were you thinking it could be?" I asked.

"I'd rather not say yet. It might put you in even worse danger if you knew and gave the game away."

"Oh Goodness, you think it's my father don't you!"

She looked genuinely surprised. "No… do you?"

"Christ, I suspect everyone. I'm so bloody scared!" I wailed, and to both our surprise, I burst into a torrent of tears.

"Hey there, girl, look, do you want to stop this charade—call it a day?" Jules asked me.

"Yes… no, oh I don't know… I'm just so afraid and I'm so tired of being frightened, y'know?"

"I do know. It was a big *ask* to expect you to impersonate

Claire and I have never liked the plan but this has to be your decision, Claire. Do you want me to call it off, tell everyone who you really are and turn this into a regular police investigation? Is that what you want? Because if it is, I will go downstairs right now and tell everyone that the real Claire is dead and that you are Nicola St. Clare, her twin sister."

Even as she spoke I knew I couldn't let her do that. I needed to be a part of this. I had to trap my sister's murderer. "No!" I told her and that was that. We agreed that I would go away for a break with my father as suggested and Jules would investigate things from another angle while we were gone.

After she left me, I got into bed with a hot water bottle and ate the hot, delicious soup that Sarah bought up to me on a beautifully prepared tray. Then I locked my door, snuggled down into my bed warm at last and slept in a deep sleep of exhaustion until the following morning, the day of my father's birthday party.

12

Lust

A family breakfast was in full swing when I came down the next morning. My father came straight to me and we hugged. I gave him my best wishes for his birthday, along with a wrapped gift that I had purchased especially for this occasion. I turned my attention to the breakfast buffet laid out upon the sideboard and was busily piling bacon and eggs onto a plate when Dennis appeared at my elbow. "What's this?" he nudged me and guffawed loudly.

"What?" I asked confused.

"Have you decided against being a despised vegetarian then?" he quipped.

I looked longingly down at the bacon lying succulently on my plate. In my hunger, I had forgotten I was meant to be a vegetarian. I thought fast. "This is for Daddy, Den, it's his birthday. I'm fixin' him a plate is all," I said, calmly.

My father called over to us, "No need, hon', I ate already. Thanks though, darlin'; come sit and watch me open my birthday gifts!"

I took some toast and piled scrambled eggs on top and then I sat down at the table and ate quickly, since I was feeling ravenous. Dennis took the plate I had originally filled and began to tuck in. I couldn't watch such was my longing for that crispy bacon. A pile of expensively wrapped parcels sat on my father's left and he begun to happily unwrap one of them. It was from Molly, and inside the plush box were a pair of beautiful monogrammed cufflinks. My father admired them and bent and whispered to Molly before kissing her fondly. The next gift was a gold pen from Dennis, then a box of cigars from Jules. Finally only my gift remained and after he opened it, my father looked across the table at me, his eyes met mine and he nodded. "Thank you," he said simply. He stood and walked around the table to kiss me.

"Land's sakes, whatever is that?" called Molly, inquisitive and peeved not to be included in this private moment. My father turned and passed her the silver frame. Molly opened it and looked at the double-sided picture frame.

"Photos?" She seemed disappointed. "How nice, Claire, and both pictures of you! Carl, you could take one of them out and put in one of you in the other side of the frame."

"No," said my father, looking at me, "both those pictures are just perfect, thank you, my darling child."

Only we two knew that one was of Claire and the other photograph was of me; both his daughters in the one frame.

The morning sped by in a hive of activity. I helped Sarah and Kate in the kitchen, making fajitas ready for the night's party. Jules kept her promise to stick by my side, so that she was roped in to help prepare food as well but she really hated cooking. She grumbled so much that Sarah, exasperated, shooed us away to help outside instead. Jules looked so smug at that, I had to laugh. We took a pile of orange and green table clothes and begun to spread them over the tables. Matt and Liam were fetching chairs and placing them around the tables. Jules began to banter with the two men, and although I smiled at the quips, I refrained from joining in. "My but you're slow workers you two!" she teased.

"Slow are we? We'll give you little girls a run for your money tonight!" Matt replied.

"Now, now, boys, we girls know you men are all the same… plenty of energy while the sun still shines but once the sun sets, well, down you go, jus' like a deflated balloon!"

"I'd say it was a case of *who* I was going down on," Liam replied with his lazy drawl.

"Liam O'Donnell, you go wash your mouth out with soap, right this instant!" Sarah snorted loudly as she came up behind him. We all watched Liam's rapid departure, his ears flaming red, Sarah hot on his tail, slapping at him with her wet dish cloth, the ribald laughter followed their retreat.

I noticed smoke coming from around the back of the house and went to investigate. The men had gotten a large barbeque going and were cooking burgers and steaks for lunch. Sarah and Kate carried out bowls of salads and plates, placing them on the table. We all queued happily and once again, I forgot my supposed vegetarian conviction and took a large steak. I wandered into the house and curled up on the sofa in front of the fire in the living room. There was no one else about inside the house and it was nice to sit in front of the crackling fire, warming me on one side, with sunlight streaming in through the windows warming me on the other. I tucked into my steak voraciously; I so missed meat. At home, I ate red meat once or twice a week. Since it had been denied me living as a vegetarian, I realised how much I missed that part of my diet. I hated the thought of eating another species but acknowledged my weakness for meat. I enjoyed it. I was a hypocrite. I knew it.

"That's steak."

My knife clattered to the floor as I jumped. Liam threw himself down next to me on the settee. I stared at him, I couldn't for the life of me think of a single thing to say in my defence. I looked at him stupidly. "It's okay, Claire, I won't tell a soul, well, on one condition," he spoke as he watched me.

"Which is what?" I asked cautiously.

"You will dance *every* dance with me tonight."

I was taken aback, I hadn't expected that. "I can't, I promised Matt a dance."

"I thought you told me you two had cooled it off?" His brows drew together in their now familiar and characteristic frown.

"Well, yeah, but…"

"That's all right then," he interrupted me; he leaned in close and told me, "you'll be my date for tonight Miss *Nicola-Claire Keedon.*"

Stupefied, I watched as he rose and left the room. I was so surprised by his use of my own name, coupled with Claire's that I hadn't even argued with him. I sat unmoving for a moment or two before leaping to my feet and racing off to find Matt to alter our plans. I was certain of only one thing; I wanted to be Liam's date that night.

I locked my bedroom door at six o' clock and ran a bath. I lay in the scented water and argued with myself about Liam. Matt had been almost relieved at my change of plan. I knew that it was foolish beyond belief to fall for anyone here on The Plomosa. After all, Liam could turn out to be my sister's killer. The trouble was, I finally admitted to myself, I found him *so very* attractive, just being around him made my stomach churn deliciously. Just thinking of kissing him… I slid under the water with a groan. I was hopeless at relationships, if my past record was anything to go by. I had had only two serious relationships in the past and both had ended rather badly. The first was with a lad I met while I was at university, Nigel. We had been an item all through university life, only splitting up at the end of our final year when Nigel asked me to marry him. I had, quite without thinking, laughed, wounding his male pride. I told him not to be so silly, I had a glittering career ahead of me and I had absolutely no intention of settling down for many years to come. Needless to say, he didn't speak to me again and at that time, I was too thick-skinned to understand why he should be so upset. I flush with shame now remembering how I must have hurt that poor young man with my callous, immature behaviour. I surfaced and swept my wet hair back from my face. After Nigel, there had been a few dates with James DeWin. James, what could one say about James? He was a law graduate, now practicing. I met him at a party one Christmas, we seemed to get along all right but he was over-polite and such a 'stick in the mud'. Of course, my mother adored him. He flirted with her outrageously and she was furious when he ended it. James was very clever, well, he would have to be to become a lawyer. Yet even his amazingly clever brain failed to work out why I behaved so badly all the while I was dating him. Mother asked me over and over what the problem had been and without going into details, I told her that he was a 'wet blanket' and that I didn't love him. Mother tried to throw us together constantly by organising parties and 'accidental' meetings. These unfortunate circumstances, which only caused acute embarrassment to both James and myself, continued until she and I had a horrendous row; one which resulted in my leaving home for good. I moved into my own flat, and I heard that James met someone more attractive and better connected than I. He married the girl six months later. I didn't get an invitation to the wedding but mother did. The galling thing was, she went to the whole event. There had been friction between us ever since. I wondered if she was missing me at all. Probably not, my mother was the type of person who had a definite 'out of sight out of mind' attitude to everyone in her life.

I realised the bathwater had cooled and so climbed out.

I spent a long time dressing, trying on this and that from Claire's wardrobe. The problem was that my bum was bigger than hers. In the end, I chose a fringed denim mini-skirt that had thin ribbon strips sown around the fringed hem in various bright colours which included lime green. I then found a lime green, sleeveless, polo-necked fitted top that matched really well with the short skirt. I pulled on a pair of pale butter-soft, suede fringed cowgirl boots. I finished the outfit with a beautiful multi coloured shawl that also had lime green within the weave. I was very conscious of how much the air chilled in the evening once the sun had gone down. After all, it had only been a few days since the blizzard had hit us. After a final twirl in front of the mirror and a swipe of Claire's pale pearl lipstick, I was done. I tapped on Jules's door but she was not quite ready, so we agreed to meet downstairs.

My father was dispensing glasses of champagne when I arrived and he waved the bottle at me invitingly, one eyebrow raised in question. "Yes, please!" I responded, reaching for a glass from the sideboard. I nearly dropped it when two hands were suddenly placed on either of my shoulders and a kiss was planted firmly on the side of my face from behind.

"Mm-hmm you smell real nice!"

"Ooh, Liam!" I exclaimed on turning.

"You were expecting someone else maybe?" He spun me around to face him and I saw his wolfish grin, his clear eyes crinkled up at the corners, head tilted to one side quizzically. I sucked in my breath, my-o-my, he was gorgeous, clean shaven for once as well. He looked sensational in black Mexican trousers, silver studs ran down the sides of the legs, he sported a fitted black Mexican shirt also with silver buttons. Lord help me tonight I thought, as my knees turned to jelly. "Nicky, Claire," he growled softly in my ear, his breath warm on my skin, "which is it tonight hmm.....hey, you okay? You look kinda... strange."

I pulled myself together. "I'm just fine, Liam. You look amazing—so dashing!" He smiled down at me and I was mesmerized, unable to look anywhere else other than into those piercing eyes of his, they seemed to see right inside my very soul.

"Claire...Claire?"

I turned my head, dazed. It was my father; he had the champagne bottle poised over the glass I was clutching. "Ooh yes, please. Happy birthday, Daddy!"

"Thanks, sweet pea. I like the outfit. You two look good together." He poured the creamy froth into my glass, as it frothed up high over the rim I lowered my head and sipped at the overflow, giggling.

"Hey, I recognise that shawl, where did you find it, hon'?"

"It was at the back of my cupboard... why?"

"I haven't seen it for a while; I gave it to your mom many years ago, is all."

"I didn't know, is it all right if I wear it—you don't mind?"

"No, honey, I don't mind in the least," he bent and kissed my cheek. He turned to Liam, looking serious all at once. "Take good care of my girl tonight, O'Donnell. See she comes to no harm and that she has a real good time."

Liam nodded, "I certainly will, sir." My father fleetingly touched my cheek with his hand and turned back to his guests.

We finished our drinks and wandered outside, it was chilly but not really cold. The temperature had risen since our ill-fated trip a week back.

The raised dais looked fabulous, the surrounding flower garlands swayed gently in the breeze. The Chinese lanterns glowed softly, illuminating every colour and every flower, so that everything came to vibrant life. The band was dressed gaily in multi-layered and coloured frilled shirts; they all wore wide sombreros, some on their heads and others were hanging behind, down their back. The melody of the music added the final magic touch. The air was pungent with a mix of barbeque smoke and candles. I was soaking up the atmosphere when a loud screech from behind us made me jump. "Darlin', where have you been?" I turned to see a vision in red, *very* low cut red. I was about to stick a smile on my face and pretend to know the vision, when to my surprise, she cast herself upon Liam and kissed his mouth with her big, red pouting lips. He, to his credit, hastily pushed her away from him and glowered at her.

"Hello, Bella," he greeted her in a low, cold voice. This could be interesting I thought and stared at Bella. She was attractive in a *very* obvious way, blonde and heavily made up. As I watched, she pouted her red lips and took Liam's arm.

"Ah, sugar, don' look at me like that, you'll make little ole me cry! Why'd you never ring me back, honey pie? Y'know you'd get a real warm welcome at ma place, baby," she purred.

I sidled backwards at this point, intending to move as far away as possible; well, I obviously wasn't needed anymore was I? Liam's arm snaked out and imprisoned my wrist. He pulled me close to his side and his arm became a steel clamp around my waist. I gasped and looked up, meeting his eyes; he winked at me and grinned engagingly. "Bella, you know we were through some eighteen months ago, so stop your games, you might upset my date. I want you to meet Miss Claire Keedon, Claire—Miss Bella Brook."

Bella looked me up and down. "We-ll, I declare the boss's daughter. Lee, darlin', *you are* goin' up in the world! Howdy do, ma'am, I'm sure."

I jerked angrily in Liam's encircling arm, I felt him pull me tighter into his side. He had no intention of letting me go. I smiled saccharine sweetly at the woman, "How do you do? It's always a pleasure to meet a friend of Liam's mom," I purred. Liam gave a bark of laughter and Bella turned an ugly shade of puce.

"Why you little bitch…" she began, but Liam interrupted.

"Now that you two girls are acquainted, why don't we go get a beer together?" Bella stuck her chin in the air and spun around wiggling swiftly away from us. Liam bellowed with laughter, stopping abruptly as I also spun away and began to stomp off. "Hey, angel, that was a brilliant put down!" he said, falling into step beside me. I stopped abruptly and turned on him.

"Go away!" I retorted.

"What… why?" he said, stunned.

"Go on, go, follow that… *that slut*!" I hissed peevishly.

"Slut?"

"*You s*aid it man!" I said, almost spitting in my anger.

"You, miss, are a jealous little witch!" Liam had hit the nail right on the head.

"I am most certainly not!" I denied, but I most certainly was.

"You are behaving like a spoilt brat, but you know *how* I deal with brats, right?"

I was seething by now and stupidly I lost it. "How dare you! I forbid you to call me a brat ever again!

Liam went very still. "You *forbid me*—is… that… so?" he asked in a deceptively velvet voice.

"Yes...that...is...right," I replied, mockingly.

"Brat," he muttered softly once again.

I raised my hand in fury, intending to slap his face. He swiftly caught it and twisted it up behind my back, pulling me hard against his chest. He bent his head and grazed my lips with his. "So *much* sexual tension," he breathed against my mouth.

Huh? I pulled back furiously. "Why you arrogant pig!"

He quelled me by pinning my arms to my sides and kissing me thoroughly. This time all the fight drained out of me. He could do whatever he liked when he kissed me like this, I melted. I was beyond caring about anything other than his delicious mouth devouring mine. Every nerve ending, every fibre of my being had turned traitor. I could not resist this man. When he finished kissing me, I was dazed and befuddled and longing for more of the same. His face softened as he gazed into my dreamy eyes. "That's so much better, come with me, you beautiful brat; I know just how to deal with you." I half -heartedly kicked at him but my heart and mind weren't in it. He chuckled huskily. "This way." His arm scooped about me and towed me along in his wake.

"Where to?" I asked, slightly nervously, I didn't trust myself to be alone with the man.

"My office," he growled. My tummy flipped, I had no option but to go with him.

His office turned out to be two rooms on the end of the dude quarters, one *was* an office with a couple of comfortable chairs and the other was a bedroom furnished simply but with a large double bed which drew my eye immediately. Liam towed me to the bed and without any preliminaries, sat down, tugging me across his knee.

Okay, I admit that I had *thought* this might happen and strangely I was looking forward to it, really weird huh? I found myself excited by the thought of a repeat performance of the spanking Liam had given me last time. I know—I know, all the fuss I made about never wanting to be spanked again, etc. etc., but I had been dreaming about him spanking me ever since that day in the cabin, and of him doing—well, more, so much more.

This time I had a skirt on and Liam flipped up the short mini and pulled my skimpy panties down below my buttocks. He stroked my rounded flesh and patted my bottom cheeks. I moaned.

"Hush, I'm gonna punish you but I'm going to make you feel so, so, good, angel." I wiggled my naked fanny and buried my face in the bed. *Whatever must he think of me?*

The first smacks came fast and light, moving from cheek to cheek, in a kind of fair play method. The burn built in a delicious way that his previous spanking had definitely lacked—last time was for punishment and had hurt. This was, well—warming and kinda sexy.

Another long moan escaped me and I heard Liam's gravelly chuckle above as he continued to heat up my posterior with light rapid swats, while I wriggled against his thigh, then I realised there was a large ridge pushing against my hip. Liam had an impressive erection. The heat from my spanked bottom began to transmit to my aching loins; I had never felt so aroused before. The staccato '*whups*' of Liam's fast hand spanking filled the room along with my moans and gasps, until finally he rested his open palm on the small of my back. I lay across his lap with my heart flip-flopping, my rear end quivering with a craven molten heat that had me totally in Liam's thrall.

When his hand slipped between my legs and his fingers dipped, exploring my intimate folds, I was shamefully abashed by the audible sounds of arousal that Liam's delving elicited. Liam gave a deep rumble of what I could only take for male appreciation and so I relaxed and enjoyed the erotic and delicious sensations that his manipulations were building. Need smouldered in my veins and anticipation surged through me as I spiralled into the free fall of orgasm. I cried aloud as I rode the crest like a surfer; on and on the pleasure took me until I reached calmer waters.

When I was back in the land of the living once more, I found myself cradled in Liam's lap. His arms were wrapped tight about me and his lips were grazing my temple.

Sighing, I snuggled into his chest. We remained that way in comfortable silence for a few minutes. I listened to his strong heartbeat and trailed my fingers up and down his sculptured biceps.

"Wow," I said softly after a while.

"Hmm," Liam replied. I sat back a little and looked up into his face.

"That was amazing, um, thank you." He studied my face and lifted a hand pushing my hair back away from my eyes. He kissed the end of my nose. It was such a cute and tender gesture, one that I had read about in books but had never experienced. A sheen of tears misted my eyes and Liam bent his head and took my lips with his, gently grazing and teasing. I shifted and felt again his hard arousal. When I moved my hand over his swollen groin and stroked, he groaned against my mouth. I slid to the floor and knelt between his legs, my hands placed on each of his open thighs. Slowly I moved a hand to his fly buttons and the huge bulge pushing against the fabric of his black Mexican trousers. Liam's hand pushed mine away and deftly he opened his fly, reached inside pulling his erection free. He was slightly larger than my two previous English boyfriends, both in length and girth; he was also circumcised which pleased me immensely. I reached for him and ran my tongue up his length. He leaned back and watched me with glittering, heavy lidded eyes. Slowly I licked around the head and then up from the base to the tip as if he were a succulent ice cream. Liam groaned—a low guttural growl. I smiled up at him letting my mouth slide over the head and sucked in his hardness, taking him deep into my warm mouth. I hummed as I suckled his throbbing shaft. I had only just begun to pleasure Liam, when he gasped and firmly pulled me upright into his arms. He took my face between his hands and kissed me, murmuring against my mouth.

"You're sure you wanna go all the way, darlin'—I do have protection—but it's gotta be your choice, my angel."

I hesitated for a moment but only because he thought that I was Claire, and I wanted him to be with me, with Nicola St. Clare—not my sister! My answer though, was to pull his black shirt loose from his trousers and glide my hands over his lean stomach, all the way up to his chest, where the plane of his muscles lay firm under my questing hands. Liam in turn, pulled my top up and off in one smooth action; he caught the skein of my hair wrapping it around his fist as it fell from the confines of my top. He tugged my head back with my hair while his free hand roamed over my breasts, popping each soft pillow from its cup. I shivered with exquisite anticipation as his head came down and suckled each nipple to attention. Liam groused as I leaned backwards to unclip my brassiere and throw it aside, thus depriving him of his soft cuddly toys. We tipped back onto the bed and he slid a hand between us seeking my slippery core, I was liquid with lust. My hand closed over his shaft and again I stroked his aching length. Liam reached behind him and produced a foil packet which he tore open with his teeth. I took the sheath from him and rolled the thing over his turgid flesh. We were so aroused that Liam simply pulled me beneath him, sliding inside me with slick precision and we were joined. He buried his head in my neck and groaned softly as he began to gyrate his hips against mine. I was wild and hungry for him as he filled me, moving and pleasuring me with thrust after deep thrust. I melded to him, cleaved to him. He braced himself onto his arms and surging his hips back, almost out of me, he slammed back into my body, pounding me until the shiver of orgasm was upon us with such a glittering intensity, it took the very breath from our bodies, leaving us with overwhelming trauma as we toppled from the pinnacle of ecstasy, Liam's mouth was seared upon mine. After a while, he moved away to lie by my side, releasing my bottom lip with a gentle nip.

I realised that up until now, I had only bedded *boys.* Liam was the first *man* I had ever made love with. I had never ever felt anything like this before. I didn't know there could be such a deep intensity of emotion coupled with lust.

Oh shit I was so screwed—literally. I stifled a giggle, I was both metaphorically and physically, screwed.

We lay exhausted upon Liam's bed, cuddling for a while. I think Liam even dozed for a bit, then he stirred and kissed me before saying, "Come on, angel, let's make ourselves presentable and go re-join the party, I want to dance with my girl." My heart did a little happy dance—Liam had called me *his girl.*

I was surprised to find that Liam had true masculine grace when dancing. He had a wonderful sense of rhythm. The band struck up with Latin music and my feet skipped. We danced palm to palm, pelvis to pelvis. It was wonderful to lose myself in dance after all the fear and worry I had suffered recently. As I spun, my body flowed with the music; I was aware of nothing and no one except Liam and the beat. At last, laughingly he pulled me from the floor and mimed and gestured with hand signals that we should go and eat. I nodded vigorously, I was ravenous by now.

The barbeque was well under way and lots of people stopped to say howdy and chat a while, so the crowd around the food was rather a crush. We managed at last to get our plates filled and Liam whispered that I could share his steak. I shook my head piously at him and he chuckled, amused no doubt by my hypocrisy. We found an empty table and sat to enjoy our meal. I had just finished eating when Matt sidled up and asked me to dance. I stood up to go with him and Liam caught my hand. He planted a kiss on my palm and let me go. On the dance floor, Matt was stiff and had none of the natural rhythm that Liam possessed. We danced but I felt awkward and uncomfortable with him and I sensed that he felt the same way. It was with some relief that I left the floor when the band finished playing. Coming towards me was Dennis holding hands with Jules, they had been dancing too. Dennis hailed me, "Claire! Excuse me, Jules, but I must dance with my sister."

I smiled at them, "Step," I said.

"Excuse me?" Dennis looked bewildered.

"Sister," I clarified, but he still looked confused.

"Step-sister!" I rolled my eyes.

"Oh-oh yeah, I see… well, who cares? We don't huh? Come on, Claire, the band is starting up again." He grabbed my hand and we spun onto the floor. He danced quite well and I had fun but I couldn't help looking around for Liam, I couldn't see him anywhere. "Thanks, sis', your dancing's improved on last year." Dennis pecked my cheek and I turned to walk off the floor, bumping straight into Liam's solid chest.

"Just where do you think you're going?" he growled, whilst spinning me around and starting another dance. I spun away from him and when our arms were full length apart he spun me back. We danced a rumba and then the band started up a tango.

The floor was almost empty and I turned to walk away, when Liam caught my elbow.

"D'you tango?" he asked.

"Oh yeah, I didn't think you would though."

"Sure I do. Come on, angel, let's show 'em how it's done!"

I put all that I had into that dance and I have to say it was the sexiest tango I'd ever danced. Liam was magnificent, full of poise and fluid motion. The tension between us was electrifying. When he flung me away, reeled me in and swept me backwards, so that I lay panting, bent almost double beneath him on that final chord; applause erupted all around us. People stamped and hooted for an encore but Liam looked at my flustered face and guided me from the floor. We went and fetched a couple of cold beers and sat down at one of the corner tables, drinking thirstily.

"Where on earth did you learn to tango, cowboy?" I finally asked; my thirst quenched.

"My ma insisted I took dancing lessons when I was a kid, after a while I kinda liked it. I wasn't bad and all the girls wanted to dance with me, so I figured it was a useful thing to be able to do."

I giggled.

"What about you? Where d' you learn to dance like that?" he asked, and without a thought, I told him the truth.

"The Finlace's School Of Dance, in Chelsea."

"Chelsea?" He looked puzzled.

I realized what I had given away and froze. *Think, Nicola, think!* "Er, yeah, Chelsea was my dance teacher. She was just so great that I wanted to be just like her when I grew up, y'know?"

Liam studied me, smiling into my eyes. "Seems to me you turned out jus' fine as you are." I blushed and let out the breath I had been holding. I had to be so careful around Liam as I naturally let my guard down with him. I must remember to think before I spoke.

A heavy hand landed on my shoulder making me jump.

"Great show, you two!" It was my father. "Well now I knew my girl was a dancer but you, O'Donnell? Where d' you learn to shuffle like that?"

Liam tipped his head to one side and a shy smile played about his gorgeous mouth. "Well, it helps when you dance with the right gal, sir." I was still mesmerised by that mouth, I knew just what it could do now.

"Just you make darned sure you're *only* Claire's dancing partner and nothing more than that!" Father said, shocking me out of my fantasy of Liam doing far more than just dancing with me.

"Hey, man… you can't speak to Liam like that!" I said furiously. My father looked somewhat stunned by my outburst.

"How much have you had to drink, my girl!" he barked sharply at me.

I was more than livid now and spun away from him, throwing over my shoulder as I stalked off, "Not as much as I *intend* to drink, you bully!" I grabbed hold of Liam's hand and towed him along beside me. After a few steps he halted and grabbed my wrist spinning me around to face him. "What?" I asked rudely with the rising temper obvious in my voice.

"Calm down, all right? It never helps to throw fuel on the fire. Your father's looking out for you; he's just protective of his little girl."

"I'm not a child anymore and it's high time he understood that!" Liam's eyes narrowed and locked mine in his steely glare. I stilled and held my breath as his hand whipped up and grasped my chin. I tingled with anticipation at the arresting sight of his tightly held jaw and forbidding scowl. *Why did it excite me that he was so cross with me*?

"Your father deserve*s* your respect and understanding. He cares about you, Claire, as do I." Liam kept my head tilted up so it was difficult to avoid his burning gaze as he awaited my reply.

"Um, yeah well, I suppose you have a point but…"

"No buts, I'm right and you have earned yourself a little trip with me, my girl!" Liam towed me in his wake and I tingled with delighted anticipation. Oh my stars, I was one *very* sick puppy. I wanted Liam to punish me, I wanted Liam to spank me, oh lordy but I had it bad. He took me back to his room, sat straight down in his upright desk chair and flung me across his knee. I fell forward and quickly put out my hands to stop myself pitching head first onto the wooden floor. For the second time that night, up went my skirt and down came my panties. Right there the resemblance to my last spanking ended. His slaps fell fast and furious all over my naked rear. I was squealing within seconds of my panties being removed. I kicked my legs and they got smacked, I wiggled my quailing bottom but that didn't help me much either. Liam kept up a rapid fire of swats that had me gasping and my eyes filling with remorseful tears.

Was this what I wanted? Did I still want this? Part of me cried NO but that wicked, sinuous little voice deep inside, the one that fell in love with spanking while watching John Wayne in *McLintock*, revelled in the delights of being punished in this time honoured way, by her strong, implacable, virile man.

The conclusion that I came to, while draped across Liam's lap, was quite simply *yes*, I wanted him to spank me. I wanted this strong charismatic man, who could really hurt me if he so wished, to take the time and the trouble to set boundaries for my behaviour. I loved knowing that he would spank me in this controlled and safe way whenever I stepped beyond them. He was showing me that he cared enough about me to enforce his own version of a safety shield about my person. I understood him and at that point of understanding, I understood me. I needed and wanted this.

By the time the last spank had fallen, I had apologised and cried tears, so that when Liam pulled me up into his lap, I burrowed in his shoulder, feeling loved and safe. Liam lectured me about my behaviour and about how I spoke to my father so very rudely and I adored it. I promised that I would apologise to my father and Liam forgave me.

Then as the 1963 Crystals song goes, '*....and then he kissed me, he kissed me in a way that I've never been kissed before, he kissed me in a way that I wanna be kissed for evermore'*.

After a breathless few minutes, Liam broke our kiss and began to talk earnestly to me. I rested my head against his shoulder; my arms wrapped around his middle and listened to the sweet rumble of his voice.

"I'm kinda old fashioned 'bout things. I think a man should be head of his household, and yet funnily enough, I'd have no problem with a wife who wants to have a career, not like some other men do."

I giggled "Ooh, how very magnanimous of you, the little woman can go out to work to earn money for your chauvinist pocket and yet the poor little thing would have no say about running her own life!" Liam chuckled and gave my bottom a playful smack.

"Stop, that's not what I meant and you know it! Hmm, let's say there was a decision to be made and neither person in a marriage can agree with the outcome, then the man should make that decision and his wife should back down and accept that he has the ultimate word. It is the best way to resolve conflict, especially in a marriage. The way I see it, it's kinda like a Chief Executive of a company, he has the final say."

"Suppose the Chief is a woman, then what?"

"In my marriage, I'll definitely be the Chief."

"You are most definitely what is currently known as, a male chauvinist pig, Mr. Liam O'Donnell."

He grinned. "And you, Miss Keedon, are what I currently call a brat. Now get up off your pretty and sore feminist butt. I'll walk you back to find your father; you owe him an apology, Miss." He stood me up and pulled up my panties. He then propelled me in front of him out of his room and across to where the party was winding down.

I noticed Matt was dancing with the girl I had met in the J.C. Penny store, I couldn't for the life of me think of her name, Laura? No—something flowery perhaps—like Lily? I simply couldn't remember. At the end of the reel, we came face to face with Matt and the girl as they stepped in front of us. "Hi, Claire, you and Leanne must catch up soon, you've not met in ages," Matt said immediately. I was grateful, he didn't think I would know Leanne, and had given me her name. I leant forward and pecked her cheek.

"How y'all doing?" I put my best drawl on. She nodded and clutched Matt's arm, giggling up at him. I cringed, she was being so obvious.

"Just fine, Claire, I hope you don't object to my monopolising Matthew, after all, y'all split up now."

I shook my head. "'Course not, we decided we weren't quite suited and broke things off a little while ago."

She looked up at Matt reproachfully; obviously Matt had neglected to mention that part.

"We're just going for a beer, want to join us?" Matt asked hastily.

"No thanks." I replied, just as Liam also said, "No, thanks all the same."

Dennis was standing drinking and chatting with a group of young men who I didn't know, there was a whistling, whining sound and a rope dropped over his head. His beer fell to the floor with a shattering of glass. Dennis grabbed the rope and pulled it hard towards him, there was an outburst of applause from the laughing crowd as Kate was pulled into sight, holding the other end of the rope. She had a big grin plastered on her pretty face as Dennis pulled her in for a big smooching kiss.

I turned to Liam, "Didn't you tell me that Kate was rehabilitated here on the ranch?"

"Yeah, she works for me in season, helping other wayward kids to reform, why?"

I stood and watched the horse play between Dennis and Kate thoughtfully. "No reason, I just wondered about her that's all."

We turned and wandered away to find my father so that I could eat some humble pie.

In the small hours of the night, I lay sleepless in my bed thinking about the evening and Liam. Why would such a gorgeous hunk like him be interested in me? He obviously hadn't been interested in Claire up until now—or had he? Was he held back from coming forward, so to speak, by Matt? It wasn't that I wasn't confident about myself, although I was realistic enough to know that I was pretty, but not beautiful. Was Liam after position, to marry the boss's daughter and improve his career prospects? I thought about the goodnight kiss we had shared and my reaction to him physically. No one had ever affected me like this before. Oh, I had enjoyed sex with both my previous boyfriends, but I had never experienced that kind of raw physical desire before. With Liam, my own existence seemed to only be possible from now onwards through the existence of him, I needed him now. I was frankly terrified of myself because I was putty in his hands and yet, he could be my sister's killer. *No!* My inner self screamed. You silly fool I argued, it could be your own murder next time around. I was just making it so easy for him. I tossed and turned, finally falling into a troubled sleep in which I dreamed of Liam spanking me and making erotic love to me. I awoke damp, sweaty and extremely frustrated.

13

Relaxed

It was with some relief that I climbed into the car the following morning. I felt as if I were leaving all my troubles behind me and I was really looking forward to a break from the ranch with my dad. It was such a relief not to have to whisper or drawl; I was entirely me again. The dogs chased us off the ranch, running behind us for a couple of miles, barking at first and then simply chasing the car. Eventually they grew bored and turned back towards the ranch.

I sat quietly absorbing and admiring the passing scenery. My father glanced sideways at me a couple of times but left me to my contemplation without so much as a word. After an hour or so of driving, I turned to him and asked, "Do you honestly believe that Liam could have killed Claire?"

He kept his eyes straight ahead and thought for a moment. "Hmm, do you mean could, or would?"

"How do you mean?"

"Well, he could have but would he have?"

"Um… I dunno… would he have?"

"Personally, I don't think Liam is our killer. Is that what you meant by the question?"

I ignored him and asked another question. "Why don't you think he killed Claire?"

"He liked her."

"Oh." My heart sank. "As in fancied her?"

"Nope, more like a kid sister."

"Ahhh." I fell silent, after a mile or two he looked around at me.

"You okay, hon'?"

"Yeah, I think so."

"So you like Liam, huh?"

"Is it that obvious?"

"Did he kiss you last night?"

"Dad!" I flushed bright red.

"Did he?"

"Uh huh."

"Did you enjoy it?"

"Enough already!"

"Nicola, did you enjoy Liam's advances?"

"Oh, all right then. Yes, look I-I like him a lot okay! I'm just worried that he's… well, you know, pretending to like me, or something. That it's about liking Claire, not me… now d'you get it?"

"Yeah, I understand. If it helps any, hon, Liam never showed the slightest attraction to Claire. Hell, poor man must wonder why he does now!"

I looked at him sharply. "You think he's guessed?"

"Oh no, no, I think he must be questioning himself as to *why*; he must be one confused cookie about now." My father chuckled. "Perhaps he put it down to your road accident with the truck, throwing you both together. I mean, he's not likely to think, hey, there must be a double who is taking Claire's place, now is he?"

"Noo, I guess not." I went back to my silent gazing. My father glanced at me a couple of times but he let me brood in peace.

We pulled into a diner for lunch and I was able to relax the vegetarian rule now that we were so far from home. "How does Molly feel about you taking off for a few days without her," I asked my father while we ate.

"She's fine about it. Den is driving her back to Vegas today. She misses her friends and she likes a little flutter now and again." I must have looked disapproving because he laughed.

"Hey it's okay, Molly's no hardened gambler. She has a little play each week with her friends and that's it." He sipped his coffee and watched me for a while. "You sure you want to carry on with this charade?" he asked me finally.

"What, run back to Liam already—no way!"

"I didn't mean *that* charade, I meant of you becoming Claire."

"Oh, I see. Well, I'm all right. I'm glad to be away from the ranch though, the strain is awful and I am so afraid all the time." He reached over and covered my hand with his own.

"You don't have to do this anymore if you don't want to. I must have been crazy to think of it. I have just found you, Nicky, and I can't stand the thought of losing you too. I am devastated to say goodbye to my Claire but I will let her go in peace, because we must build a life together you and I, as father and daughter."

"Thank you, but I want to carry on with this and see it through, for Claire's sake as well as for you too. I'll be okay. This is what I need, a break from the strain and worry and a chance to get to know my father without the stress of being my twin." I smiled at him.

"I'm looking forward to having you all to myself as well and getting to know more about you. Although, we have come such a long way in such a short time don't you think?" I assured him that I did and settled back, determined to enjoy my meat meal. After finishing our coffee, I went to the restroom while he paid the bill. On the road again, I noticed that we were climbing and it was getting much colder.

"Where exactly are we going?" I asked.

"I don't suppose I'll be able to keep my secret much longer because there'll be signs up giving it away soon. Okay, Nicky, we are going to the Grand Canyon." I stared at him delighted.

"Wow, that is just amazing, so cool!"

You're really pleased?"

"Absolutely. I've always wanted to go there—well, who wouldn't? I never believed that I would though. Wow, when will we get there… is it much further?"

He gave a bellow of laughter. "You sound so like Claire when she was six, I bet you were exactly the same! Only another hour or so of driving to go, I'm so glad you're pleased."

"I can't wait; this is so groovy thank you so much!"

"Honey, you're very welcome and we're gonna have a great time!"

I leaned over to kiss his cheek, before settling back into my seat hugging myself with glee. To relax and enjoy myself free from the choking fear that had become so much a part of everyday life seemed an impossible treat, and it was one that I fully intended to relish.

We began to climb and as we did, the temperature dropped. We stopped to pull jackets on over our sweaters and drank hot coffee from the flask, walking about and stamping our feet to keep warm. The car heater was somewhat temperamental.

I noticed that there was still snow lying on the ground between the trees and I wondered if there would be more snow higher up. There was. Not a huge amount but the ground was covered in white with just the odd dark patch of ground here and there.

I loved this wild country, so different to the safe and tame picture postcard prettiness of the English countryside. Here the beauty was uncultivated, capacious. Land as God had intended it to be.

I asked if the forest we were travelling through had a name,

"Yup," replied my father, "this here is the Kaibab National Forest and it covers the land all the way to the Grand Canyon rim."

"Cool."

I must have nodded off because when I awoke, we were slowing at a sort of check point manned by a man wearing a uniform. My father lowered his window.

"Good afternoon, sir, welcome to the 'Grand Canyon National Park... Oh, it's you, Mr. Keedon sir, hello!"

I realised that the man must be a Park Ranger.

"Hi, Joe, how's things?" my father asked him.

"I'm just fine thank you, sir and yourself?"

"I'm very well thanks, Joe. My daughter and I are taking a little vacation together."

"Staying at the C.K.?"

"Nope we're staying right in the Village this time, having ourselves a real break from the office."

"Well you have a great time, sir. Just so you know, sir, North Canyon Road is still closed... snow."

"Yup, I thought it might be, well, be seeing you, Joe."

The Ranger tipped his hat and stepped back from the car allowing us to drive on through the check point.

The road continued to climb and then levelled out. I gazed about me hoping to see the canyon but there were spruce trees lining the road edge obscuring the view.

There were signs up, North Canyon pointing in one direction and South Canyon the other. The North Canyon sign had a large red 'closed' sign stuck over the top. We drove on until buildings appeared and my father turned off. I was surprised and disappointed at the number of cars and buildings, it was much more commercial than I had expected. When I voiced my surprise at this, my father merely smiled and nodded saying, "Just wait and you'll see why people come here, hon."

We checked in at the reception area of the El Tovar Hotel and dumped our suitcases inside with the bellboy before returning to the car once again. My father pulled off and drove slowly to another parking area. "Right, hop out." I did as he bid and followed him through trees onto a wide and well-trodden pathway. The trees fell away suddenly and a wave of warm air rushed over my face.

Staring at what lay before me, I sucked in my breath and gasped, "Oh my God!"

Beside me my father chuckled delightedly. "D'you know *every single* person says that when they see this amazing view for the first time."

I didn't doubt it because before me lay another world. A world of light and dark pink striped rocks laced with green shadows, a space so huge it simply beggared belief. The rock face fell away steeply at our feet and dropped downwards well over a mile below. On the chasm's floor, a pink Colorado River snaked its sinuous and curving way along the bottom of the ravine. Large birds hung suspended above the enormous space, floating on thermals of warming air as it rose high above the canyon. This ancient prehistoric place had its own characteristic smell and quality of being. I was simply spellbound. It took some time for my brain to accept the vastness of the space involved. Awe made me speechless after my first exclamation of amazement. I dropped to my haunches on the ground and simply sat, staring at the phenomenon that is the Grand Canyon.

After a while, my father placed his hand on my shoulder. "Nicky?"

"Mmm."

"Time to go, hon, there will be plenty of time to see more later. Let's go see our Lodge and get settled."

I sighed, reluctant to tear my eyes away from the beauty before me, but when my father offered me his hand I took it and rose to my feet following him reluctantly back to the car.

"Is the canyon as you expected it to be?" he asked eagerly once we were seated in the car.

"Crumbs no, I never expected it to be *pink* for a start and it's so huge! The drop down to the bottom is so deep and so sheer! I thought it would be yellow and like a desert, y'know, all sandy and beige looking."

"I know. Did you know this is the only place in the world that you find pink rattle snakes?"

"No, really… *pink*?"

"Yeah, amazing isn't it?"

We looked at each other, our eyes shining and laughed. "Thank you for bringing me here to this truly amazing place," I said simply, and leant towards him.

We embraced and he groaned, "Oh, Nicola, I am so sorry about everything, darlin', how can you ever forgive me for this mess."

I drew back and looked at him. He had tears in his eyes. "Hey, Dad, it's okay, really it is."

"No, Nicola, I've wronged you all… Claire, your mother and yourself. I insisted on the parting of the two of you as babes. I was arrogant and selfish and terribly wrong, I shall never forgive myself, not ever."

"I forgive you for both of us, Dad," I told him quietly. "We won't talk about it anymore, let's just enjoy our special time together and forget the past for a while."

"Nothing you say can change how I feel, just as I can't undo what has already been done." He sighed and nodded curtly to emphasise his point then started the car, saying as we pulled away, "We still have more to talk about and I want to know why you are so angry with your mom."

I nodded and sat back resigned, wondering how to put that question's answer into words. I was so angry with my mother that articulating my fury seemed an impossible task. How to explain her interference in my life? The controlling, the manipulation and finally the deception. She was a selfish woman, a beautiful woman, one used to getting her own way all of the time. I glanced at my father, he was a handsome man, a strong willed man and, I knew, a ruthless man. How else had he built up a multimillion dollar business? Yet he saw and regretted his mistakes in a way that my mother did not. How to explain any of this to him, so that he understood the raw wounds that ran deep and painful within me? My thoughts were interrupted by the visual stimulus of the canyon village. There were rustic log lodges with parking areas, a restaurant and shop. We pulled up outside the El Tovar Hotel lodge and went inside.

A wide foyer decorated with buffalo horns and Indian artefacts greeted us, while a ceiling fan hummed overhead, stirring the air pleasantly. We collected our keys and made our way up a large central staircase to our room. We had a suite, comprised of a large central sitting room with a bedroom off each end of the room and ensuite bathrooms off each bedroom. I gasped with delight when I saw the views from the windows. Our rooms faced the canyon and looked right over the enormous ravine.

A young man appeared with our bags and my father tipped him before turning to me and asking, "Okay then, which bedroom d'you want, hon?"

I ran from room to room delighted with both rooms and finally decided on the one with a spectacular picture of the canyon at sunset placed above the huge bed. There were pictures of the canyon in all its facets dotted around the suite but the sunset was glorious.

"You just wait 'till you see a sunset for yourself. That picture on the wall is only a taste of what you'll see," my father assured me.

We ate in the hotel restaurant and returned early to our rooms. It had been an exhausting day and we were both so fatigued, that we said our goodnights and turned in early.

I awoke early the following day and sat curled in a chair watching the mists clear from the canyon below, the bright rays of golden sunlight chased away the shroud that hid the Grand Canyon's ancient magnificence beneath.

I turned and smiled as my father appeared by my side, his hand lightly squeezing my shoulder in greeting. Silently we watched the magic unfold; companionably we drifted away to shower and dress when the dazzle of the sun streaming into the room made it impossible to withstand the glare any longer.

After breakfast, my father wanted to visit the Watch Tower at Desert View Point and I agreed to go with him, although I really wanted to walk the rim and savour the place on foot.

We drove along the East Rim towards the Desert View point and to the Watch Tower, I was thrilled to be able to spot the Colorado River twisting its pink migration along the depths of the gorge. At the Watchtower, we parked and walked, agreeing to meet up at the View Point after looking around on our own. I loved the way the Tower fit in so well with its environment despite being only a re-creation of the unusual towers built by the Indians so long ago. I was following a group of people up some steps when my eye fell on the back view of a man standing below. My breath caught in sudden shock. I was certain; it was him. He was wearing one of the chequered shirts that he favoured so much. The woman in front of me turned to stare and I realised that I had spoken aloud the chant which was swelling in my head. "Oh God no, not him, *please lord don't let it be him*," but I knew in my heart that it was.

14

Suspicion

I found my father gazing through a telescope at the river below, and as he turned, his smile of greeting died. He hurried over to my side. "What's wrong?" he asked urgently.

"The murderer, I know who he is!" My mouth felt stiff and awkward as I spoke.

"Who, Nicola, *who is it*?"

"It's Liam, Dad. I know that it's Liam."

We sat in a cafeteria sipping coffee, all conversation had died. My father had tried unsuccessfully to convince me that the man I had seen was not Liam and I had equally *unsuccessfully* tried to convince him that it was. After a while my father spoke, "This is ridiculous, Nicky girl, we can't let this spoil our break together. I suggest we head off in the opposite direction and walk a bit around the rim, what do you say?"

"Yeah whatever," I replied, still cross with him for not believing me.

"Listen to me, young lady, an attitude adjustment is required right now or very shortly you will find yourself face down over Daddy's knee, comprendre?" I swallowed and felt my cheeks flush with embarrassment as the raw memory of being across Liam's knee shattered my soul. It was one thing to be in *that* situation with a man you fancy, but quite another when contemplated by your father!

"Please answer me, daughter mine, before I take action here and now." My father spoke firmly but quietly and I gasped as he laid his hand over my wrist and gripped it warningly.

"Yes, I understand!" I spoke hurriedly, hearing the slight nervous shake in my voice as I answered him, because I sensed that he would have no compunction about taking me across his knee in a public place. Hell, I knew he would do it too, just to make his point.

"Now then, Nicola, would you like to go down into the canyon?" he asked me.

My head shot up; he had my attention now. "Can we, but how?"

"Various ways—by helicopter maybe?"

I shook my head. I had only once flown by helicopter and that was after our truck accident. I had felt extremely sick; it was not an experience I cared to repeat any time soon. Again another memory of Liam and yet another spanking recollection!

"Okay, by mule then?"

Now he was talking.

"Yeah, that would be fantastic! Do we hire the mules or what?"

"You would need to sign up for the trip with a Mule Train and stay overnight at the Phantom Ranch."

"The what?" I interrupted him.

"Phantom Ranch, it's called that because it's not in use all year round. It's just for tourists not a real ranch. We can go and book you up for tomorrow right now if you like."

"What's with the 'you'? It's us."

"No, no, hon, I'm too old for mule trekking. Besides I need to call into the Canyon C.K. and check all's well."

"Hey, you said no work on this trip, Dad, remember?" I was disappointed.

"I know, but if you are happy and busy, it won't hurt if I just check in, will it?" he wheedled.

"Dad, this is not because we argued is it?" I still didn't know him well enough yet to understand his moods.

"What? Heck no, honey. I just couldn't sit on a mule all day is all! My old butt wouldn't take the punishment. I'm jus' fine dishing it out, I just can't take it!" He winked and I had to laugh.

"Well, if you're sure you won't mind being alone for the next couple of days, I really would love to go."

"Come on then. What are we waiting for—let's go get you booked in!" In any event, I couldn't get in on the 'train' the following day and so I was booked for the day after that.

The next day, I decided to take a hike alone around the canyon's rim. I wanted to take some time to mull over everything that had happened to me over the last couple of months. We had booked my mule train adventure for the day after. Meanwhile, today, my father had gone over to his C.K. Motel to check over a few things with the manager there. I didn't mind that he was working, since I needed space to clear my head.

I walked for a couple of hours, taking the time to rest occasionally and sip water from my canteen; it was such a relief to be alone with my thoughts.

As the day progressed, the calmer I became. The views from the rim were simply mind blowing. I had my trusty Leica with me and I tried to capture the essence of the place, using the amazing light and shadow that played across the prehistoric basin below. The day passed more quickly than I expected and before long, it was time to return to the hotel and join my father for dinner.

We chattered nonstop over our meal and I felt that, by the time we made our way up to bed, I knew him a little better. He was familiar to me now and I was relaxed in his presence. Carl Keedon was starting to feel like *my* Dad.

As we assembled for the mule train, I was pleasantly surprised by my group of fellow travellers. They were a mixed but friendly bunch of people, a couple of Australians, a couple of Scandinavians too. Obviously older tourists were as conscious of their aging backsides as my father had been of his; I would have said that there was no one in our group over the age of forty except our guide perhaps. He looked fairly ageless under his hat but I guessed him to be in his early forties. We were being given instructions on the handling of our mules, when our guide hailed a late comer to the party. I was bending down checking the girth on my mule, who was called Harris, when a familiar voice by my side startled me.

"Claire, howdy, darlin', I didn't realise you were gonna be here!"

I straightened up, slowly, with a sickening sense of betrayal. "Hello, Liam, what are you doing here?" *As if I didn't know.*

"Hey, angel, aren't you surprised to see me?"

Oh the injured innocence portrayed on that handsome but treacherous face.

"No, I spotted you yesterday at the Watch Tower. I knew then that you were following me." Liam quirked his eyebrow and a confused look crossed his rugged face.

"Huh? I simply took my leave as planned. I have two new teens starting at the end of May and since your father was on vacation, I thought I'd come on up here. It's been three years at least since my last visit and I just fancied spending some canyon time. It kinda gets into your blood, if you know what I mean. How 'bout you? You never said you were coming to the Grand Canyon. Your father suggested he was taking you to Vegas with him, is he here too?" He looked around for my father.

"Yeah, we came here first. He's not coming on the mule train though—excuse me, I have to mount up now." Everyone was climbing up onto their mules amid excited chatter and some laughter.

"Hey, let me help you there." Before I could even protest, he had lifted me into the air and I was astride my mule. He turned and pushed through the merry throng, stopping to exchange small talk with the group as he made his way, leaping agilely up onto his own grey beast. I ground my teeth with muted fury and urged Harris to follow the others who had begun to move forwards and down the trail. At least I should be safe from Liam if I stayed tight within the group. My pleasure evaporated just like dew on grass in warm sun and a sense of dread began to fill me as we descended the steep and winding trail. I would need to be extremely vigilant if I were to survive the next two days.

I would like to have gazed outwards at the amazing views across the canyon but it took all my concentration to follow the stony trail and keep my eye on Liam. I knew that he was about seventh in the line of people in front of me and I intended to keep it that way. The entire group numbered twelve, including the guide.

When we stopped for a water break, it was difficult to get Harris moving again; before I knew what was happening, Liam was beside me urging the stubborn creature forward. I thanked him stiffly but then ignored him. My heart was hammering uncomfortably, knowing that my possible killer was now following my tail behind me.

By noon, I was ready for a break, and it was a relief to find shade to rest in. Although it was still rocky, the path had widened out and when I looked down, it seemed we were not far from the canyon's stony floor. I sat under a rocky overhang with my side to the rock while I ate my soft cheese roll; I was slightly apart from the other folk. Liam sat chatting with the trail boss and totally ignored me. I was strangely peeved by this.

It was hot, so much warmer than up on the rim above. As the sweat dripped into my eyes, I wished that I had not come on this trip but then I chided myself for such wimpish behaviour. It rankled with me that Liam seemed to be having such a great time. He was chatting up all the women and totally ignoring me; well that was a good thing wasn't it? Good grief what was wrong with me? The sun must have pickled my brain or something—I mean anyone would think I was jealous!

Harris must have sensed my absent minded mood because the next thing I knew, there was a thump in my lower quarters and I was sailing through the air over the edge of the trail and falling, falling down towards the canyon below. It was a few seconds before the realisation of what had actually happened flooded my brain, and then in blind panic, I flung out my arms to try and grab onto something, *anything,* to stop myself going down. I was lucky, my hand struck the rock side, painfully, but I scrabbled and grabbed at the solid rock face and held on. My arms were suddenly wrenched by the settling of my body weight. My grip held good as I swayed gently to and fro, the tendons and muscles in my arms screamed with the effort of holding my own body weight. My fingers ached while digging into the sharp surface of the rock face. I screamed and screamed. Mercifully, I heard Liam's voice drifting down to me and I dared to slowly lift my head and look skywards.

"Hold on, angel, I'm coming down, just hold on there!" It seemed an eternity before a rope dropped beside me and I reached a hand out to grip it, then a scattering of soil and debris fell past me tumbling down and onwards. I felt sick. The reassuring presence of another human arriving by my side was an enormous relief, causing tears to spill unchecked down my face. It was Liam all roped up and I was never so glad to see anyone as of that moment. I didn't stop to think of the danger he might present towards me, I instinctively trusted him. "Look at me, Claire, keep your eyes focused on my face and keep holding onto that rope. I want you to trust me now and do *everything* that I tell you, baby, okay?"

"Yes," I whispered.

"I'm going to rope you up and then I'll guide you back up as you are being raised up to the top, you got that?" I nodded my head since I was unable to speak owing to the fact my teeth were chattering with fear. My shoulders were screaming, tearing with the pain from holding my weight for so long. Liam quickly and efficiently tied ropes around and under me before signalling with a tug on the line that we were ready to go up. "Okay, darlin', place your feet on the rock in front of you and walk yourself up the rock face, like this." He demonstrated for me. "Come on, angel, you can do this!" Slowly and gradually we crept upwards towards the safety of the ridge. When we finally reached it, I was lifted by strong arms and helped to safety as far back from the edge as it was possible to be. A blanket was dropped around my shoulders and someone passed me a flask of water to drink and then he was there. Liam hunkered down beside me and gathered me to him, pressing his lips to my forehead. I burrowed into his chest with shuddering sobs and hung onto him for all I was worth.

"You're safe now, Claire, you're safe, darlin', it's okay I'm here-I'm here." Just like that I no longer feared him for I knew him and I can't explain it better than that. *I just knew him and I knew that I was his. The question was would Liam want me?*

MY FATHER WAS absent when we arrived back at the hotel, which was a relief because I think he would have fussed over much and we needed time to talk.

Liam ran me a hot bath, placing me in the warm water and lifting me out afterwards. He wrapped me in a fluffy white towel and sat himself down in one of the comfortable arm chairs with me cradled on his lap. "I want to know what's going on, Claire. You have to tell me everything now or there can't be a future for us as a couple." I sighed in frustration, I couldn't share my impersonation of Claire with Liam, the knowledge could be too dangerous and this was far more than just my personal secret. Would Liam even believe that I wasn't Claire?

"I do want to tell you everything, Liam, I do but please be patient with me. There is so much at stake here and the secrets are not all mine to share."

"Ah, so there is something going on, I knew it. Look I want you to be my girl, Claire, and maybe someday we'll marry and have children together, but a relationship like that has to be based on trust. But if you feel that you can't trust me, then I have to walk away, darlin', and I so *do not* want to do that. Just trust me, angel, tell me what's going on, I just want to keep you safe." I shifted, uncomfortable with the direction this conversation was taking.

"Liam, I think I'm falling in love with you and I really want to be with you too, but there is something that I have to finish before I can come to you… and well, you might not want me after you know what is going on. I do trust you, but believe me when I tell you that it really is unimportant right now. My life has to be put on hold, just for a little while longer, so please just wait for me and in turn, just trust me. Do you think you can you do that?" Liam pressed a sweet kiss on my forehead and lifted me in his arms, turning he gently placed me down into the chair and turned towards the door.

He looked back over his shoulder sadly. "I want you for my wife, Claire, but there has to be trust on *both* sides for that kind of commitment, darlin'." He left quietly, closing the door behind him. I sat without moving and played back our conversation over and again in my head, before I crumpled and wept bitter tears of heart break and self-recrimination. Even if I told him the truth eventually, would this handsome cowboy, with his complex character and deeply ingrained integrity, so full of old fashioned values, still want me, especially when he found out the depth of my deception?

I pulled on my pyjamas and snuggled into bed. I had brought Claire's diary with me, not wanting to leave it where someone searching might too easily find it. I would finish it tonight and perhaps it would answer some of the questions churning around in my head.

15

Resolve

My bedroom door cracked open at about one o'clock in the morning and my father stuck his head around the doorway. "I wasn't expecting you back tonight, what happened?" he asked me, wandering into my room and perching on the side of my bed. I filled him in on the whole terrifying mule episode and my subsequent conversation with Liam. I told him that I wanted to travel to Las Vegas and the C.K. Motel Casino to visit Dennis. I didn't tell him why and he didn't ask, but he did agree that we should leave first thing in the morning. He tucked me in as though I was a small child and kissed my forehead sweetly, wishing me goodnight. He switched off my table lamp and crept softly from the room.

I had finally finished reading Claire's diary. Her suspicions that the books were crooked and being fiddled at the casino were well founded. According to the diary, money laundering on a large scale appeared to have been going on for the same period of time that Dennis had worked there. Claire suspected fake losses and fake wins were being used to launder money through the casino and she was convinced that Dennis had to have known about it. I needed to speak to Dennis, but I also realised that it was probable Dennis was Claire's killer. I had to be so very careful. I decided that I would not involve my father until I had spoken to Jules.

Before we checked out the following morning, I phoned the ranch and left a message for Jules to meet me in Vegas. I left a note explaining everything to Liam and I asked the concierge at the reception desk to make sure that he received it urgently.

THE DRIVE to Vegas was quiet and uneventful. My father and I were each lost in our own thoughts and we travelled in companionable silence for most of the way.

The only exception was his curiosity about the relationship that I had with my mother. I tried to explain her emotional neglect of me. He, in turn, shocked me by telling me how hard she had fought him over keeping both Claire and I together as babes.

He told me that twice she had flown out to America to visit Claire. The first time was when Claire had been three-years-old and she had fallen from the top of the stairs to the bottom. Knocking herself out cold in the fall, she had remained unconscious for nearly a week. My mother had flown out and slept beside her bedside until Claire had opened her eyes and been declared out of danger.

The second time was her at college graduation, where, like my father when he came to my graduation ceremony, she remained hidden within the crowds of families and well-wishers. Perhaps I had been too hard on my mother, a woman who had had her child wrenched from her and who probably lived with the guilt of the choices she made that led up to that heart breaking circumstance. I certainly had a lot of food for thought on my journey to America's 'Sin City'.

We arrived late and so I was able to see the amazing lights on the 'Strip' and the completely over the top architecture that is Vegas. The whole place was buzzing due to Elvis Presley's and Pricilla Beaulieu's wedding, which had taken place on the first of May, only the previous day. Carefully negotiating the crowded streets, we finally turned into a small quiet road; my father drove down into an underground car park situated at the back of the motel.

The casino was in full swing when we walked inside. There were some sickly looking people hooked up to the many one-armed bandits, their faces a white, greenish tinge, partly from the lights but also from fatigue. I was not impressed with my first ever visit to a gambling house. Dennis seemed to be frantically busy and so I figured it was a bad time to tackle him. Besides, I wanted to wait until Jules arrived for support and advice.

She arrived at about three in the morning. After she read Claire's diary entry, she sat still and quiet, thinking. I made us both some tea and waited for her conclusion. She made me jump and spill my tea when she finally broke the silence. "I think we need to confront him alone just the two of us. I'm going in armed, Nicola, and I want you to do exactly what I tell you at all times, got that?" I nodded wide eyed. Then she pulled up her sweater to reveal a Smith and Wesson .38 strapped to her torso.

"Oh my God," I groaned. This was all becoming far too real for me.

Jules glanced my way and shrugged. "It was bound to get nasty sooner or later." I stood up, swallowed nervously and followed her as she left the room.

We found Dennis alone in his office. Jules pushed me in through the door and waited outside hidden behind the wall. I left the door wide open so that she could hear everything said within the room. If Dennis was surprised to see me at this hour of the morning, he didn't show it. He looked up, smiled and offered me a drink. I politely declined. "Well then, to what do I owe this pleasure, sis?" he asked.

I took a deep breath. "I know that you are laundering money, Dennis, and I know how. What I don't know is why? Isn't what my father pays you enough?"

His smile slipped and his mouth twisted. "You want the truth? Well, he treats me like a fucking lackey! I get peanuts running this place. When the syndicate asked me, *oh so nicely*, to run money through the casino while paying me a good cut, not only had I no choice but you know what, Claire, I wanted to do it—just to screw your father over!"

I blanched at his hatred and as he stepped forward pushing his face into mine. I took a faltering step backwards. "Why Dennis? What did he ever do to you?" I asked.

"I told you—I'm manager in name only, your father won't let me make any decisions or make changes, hell I can't even fire staff without his fucking say so… and you… his fucking little princess. The pair of you make me sick to my stomach!" *The pair...so it was Dennis!*

"It was you. You killed my sister, Claire!" I felt the bile rise up into my throat.

"What the—you're fucking nuts—you are Claire!"

"I'm Nicola, *her twin sister*, you murdering bastard!" Incoherent molten fury swept through me and I launched myself onto him, pummelling him with my fists. To his credit, Dennis didn't hit me back. He simply covered his face as I attacked him, berserk with rage.

Into this furore came Jules, gun drawn, voice cold. "That is enough—I said—Stop, Nicola!" She grabbed my shoulder and spun me away from Dennis, her gun pointed directly at him.

He put his hands up in the air and grinned at her. "Hey, you got me, Jules, what can I say?"

Jules reached behind her and pulled out a pair of handcuffs. "Put these on him, Nicky." Dennis held out his wrists and I snapped on the cuffs. This had gone so much better than I thought it would.

"Okay, I have the car down below, let's go—Move!" She shoved Dennis forward and I followed her, feeling relief that it was all finally over. "I need you to come with me to the precinct, Nicky… you okay?" I nodded and murmured an affirmative.

We made our way to the underground car park unseen and Jules unlocked the car, pushing Dennis into the back seat. "Will you sit in the back too and keep an eye on him for me?" she asked me. Agreeably, I climbed in beside Dennis on the passenger side. Jules climbed into the driver's seat with Dennis sitting behind her. She started the car and drove out into the dark street. Dawn wasn't far off and the sky was beginning to lighten. I looked at Dennis and found him studying me closely.

"So where did you come from all of a sudden?" he asked.

"From England, Claire and I were split up by our parents when their marriage failed and my mother took me back to the U.K. with her; Claire stayed here with our father."

"Jeez, it's like that film, y' know the one… err," Dennis paused, thinking.

"*The Parent Trap*, Hayley Mills?" I filled in for him.

"Yeah-yeah, I remember that. So why don't I know about you?"

"I didn't know about any of this until after you murdered Claire!" My voice was rising again; I must try and stay calm.

"Me? You think I killed Claire? Jules—hey, are you hearing this?"

I interrupted before Jules could reply. "Was it Kate… you and Kate? Did she lasso Claire off Sasha and throttle her to death?"

"Kate—what the—No. How do you even know that Claire is dead? I mean she could be hiding out somewhere!"

"I saw her body, you bastard! I saw what you and that bitch did to my twin!" I lashed out and caught Dennis a blow on his mouth. A trickle of blood ran down his chin, the sight of his cut lip staying my hand, and I lowered it to my lap. I was shaking badly but I would not become like him. Dennis was scrutinizing me closely and I turned my head quickly to one side, allowing my curtain of hair to fall and cover my face. I couldn't bring myself to look at him, I was too distraught.

After a few moments of tense silence Dennis spoke again in a low voice, "I'm sorry, okay. I didn't know about Claire. I swear it wasn't me that killed her. Was it you, Jules? I would never have agreed to run cash for your bosses, if I'd known what you lot were capable of!"

Say what! I spun back to look at Dennis—*what the—Jules?*

"Shut your mouth, you fool. You don't know what the fuck you're talking about! The stupid bitch was gonna bring us all down. She had to go. I had no choice in the matter, orders from above you wouldn't want to ignore."

"So where the fuck are you taking us now? Gonna kill us too?"

I gasped and looked out of the car window; we were heading out into the desert and away from town and any police presence. I realised that the bravado Dennis had shown was because he knew that he was safe with Jules. He had been acting all along, they both had. The handcuffs in front of his body and not behind his back, it was all making sense to me now. How naive and trusting I had been with them both.

After that, things became blurred, everything happened so fast that it's hard to remember the exact order of events. I think Dennis yelled, "The gun!" Jules stretched her hand out to the front passenger seat where she had placed the .38 when she first jumped into the car. I leapt forward pushing my hand between the seats and then I grabbed her wrist, stopping her. Dennis flung his handcuffed arms over her head and pulled her up and backwards by the throat. The car began to swerve violently out of control as Jules clawed at Dennis's arms. I know I was screaming at that stage and then—well nothing.

I woke up in a hospital bed with my father and Liam standing over me and a doctor flicking a pencil light in and out of my eyes. "Welcome back, my dear, how are you feeling?" the doctor asked while he held my wrist in his fingers and took my pulse. My mouth felt like sandpaper. You know, I've read that in books before and it's actually a really good description because that is *exactly* how my mouth felt. I tried to speak but groaned. The doctor gestured to the water by my bedside and Liam jumped up and helped me to sip from the glass. I noticed how tired and unshaven he looked and I wondered how long I'd been here.

"How long?" I managed to croak.

"How long have you been here? Twenty-four hours, my dear. Now then, I need to ask you a few questions before I allow the police in, they are most anxious to question you, do you understand?"

"Yes," I nodded.

"What is your name?" the doctor asked.

I tried to smile. "Depends who I'm talking to," I answered flippantly. Liam and my father both growled softly at me. I grinned and then regretted it, my lips were so sore that I gasped.

The doctor patted my arm. "You have facial abrasions, my dear, superficial but painful nonetheless. Let us try again shall we? Your full name please."

I sighed. "Nicola St. Clare." Something dawned on me. "Ooh, is that how my mother chose between us—Claire St. Clare, well I mean she'd sound like a saint wouldn't she?" My mother had to choose which baby to take back to England with her. Knowing that she planned to take her maiden name as her surname after the divorce, she chose me because in the 'lucky dip' of names, I was Nicola. Had I been the twin named Claire, I would probably have been the dead twin. I shuddered, fate was a fickle friend.

The doctor shook his head at me. "Concussion I think."

"No," my father interrupted him, while smiling at me sadly. "She *is* making sense, I understand what she's saying, please continue, doctor."

After answering the entire list of doctor's questions relating to the month, *May*, the year, *1967*, the President, (that took some thinking about being English), *Lyndon Johnson*. The doc declared me fit for police questioning and released me to return home.

"SO LET me get this straight. Jules was a legit police officer in Vegas but she also worked for this crime syndicate that pressured Dennis to launder money through the C.K. casino?"

Chief Stewart nodded. "Yes, I'm real sorry. It doesn't happen very often but when a cop goes bad, we all feel the disgrace throughout the service, ma'am. I'm sorry that Danker died in the car crash and won't face justice for the murder of your sister."

"You are *sure* it was her and not Dennis who killed Claire?" Dennis had survived the crash and was 'helping the police with their inquiries but I still found it hard to believe that Jules Danker was the killer and had made attempts on my own life. I had genuinely liked her. "Why did she try to kill me if she already knew that I wasn't Claire?"

"Smoke and mirrors to throw you and everyone else off her scent; they were half-hearted attempts, made only to frighten you. Danker could have killed you any time she wanted. I think she believed that you would give up and go home. Then the case would just remain unsolved, after all who would suspect a cop?"

"But why *kill* Claire, Mr. Stewart; after all it was only money."

Stewart gave a harsh laugh. "Hmm, more crime is committed in this world for 'only money' than for any other reason, young woman. Your sister realised that the sum of money going in and out of the casino didn't tally up, so she spoke to Dennis and Dennis tried to shut the whole operation down. The syndicate obviously weren't too happy 'bout that and sent Danker to meet secretly with Claire. Your sister thought she was safe meeting with a police officer. We think they rendezvoused at Iron Canyon, your sister on horseback and Danker by helicopter. The records show she booked the rescue Huey out on the day of your sister's murder. Danker landed the helicopter on Pinto Rock, which is just wide enough and flat topped, perfect for landing a 'copter. She strangled your twin sister and took off, leaving no tracks behind, except your sister's going in or out of the canyon. It all hangs together. I can only say that I'm real sorry, Miss St. Clare." He stood up indicating the interview was over, I shook his hand and went out into the hallway where Liam awaited me.

We hadn't had a chance to talk properly, or be alone since the accident, for want of a better word to describe what had happened that awful night. I noticed how warily he watched me and he was so polite around me, but then, today was the first time that we been together without my father present. He had allowed Liam to drive me into see Chief Stewart today to go over my police statement. My father needed to be with Dennis and Molly while Dennis consulted with his attorney at law.

After we left the building, Liam took my arm and guided me to a small restaurant across the street where we ordered lunch. Liam waited until the waitress had taken our order before opening up the difficult conversation that we needed to have. "So then, secrets…"

I watched him nervously, awaiting his condemnation and judgement. "I guess you felt unable to share yours with me because involving me might have put me in harm's way, am I right?"

I let out my breath. "Yes *exactly*… oh Liam, you have no idea how difficult this whole thing has been. I, well, I just didn't expect to fall in love on top of…" *bloody hell—I just told the man I loved him*! I froze and waited—a rabbit in headlights.

Liam winked at me and reached his hand out across the table placing it over mine. "Hey, that's okay, I kinda like you too, Nicky St. Clare."

Epilogue

1970

The start of a new decade and of a new life, our daughter, Tabitha Claire O'Donnell, was born on January the sixth, 1970. She is the spitting image of her father, with a thatch of chestnut hair on top of her sweet head. Liam swears that she is the double of me but I think that is because she has enormous blue eyes.

My mother was here for the birth and Molly and my father are flying up to California at the weekend.

Liam and I moved to California to help set up a reform ranch that caters for twenty or so youngsters between the ages of twelve and sixteen. We both love our work and I have just completed my diploma, which enables me to carry out family assessments. My learning has been invaluable to me especially in helping me to build a new and stronger relationship with my mother.

Dennis was given an eight year jail sentence for his crimes and my father sold the C.K. Motel chain and officially retired, giving me a trust fund that enabled us to buy our home in California. He still runs the tourist dude side of the ranch but the discipline part left with Liam and me after we were married.

I dream of Claire now and again and my father and I talk of her often. I feel closer to her now and I feel that she is finally at peace.

Liam has been my rock and oh how I love that man, especially when he spanks my sassy British behind—yeah—I have to say life is good.

JOSIE CLOSED the diary and stared into space. Why had she not known any of this? Her mother had never told her a thing about her dead aunt, or the drama surrounding her death. Why had no one told her? Her phone chirruped, she glanced at it, Max again. Josie tapped her teeth with her nail thoughtfully. Coming to a decision, one that she thought her grandmother Nicola would approve of, she punched in 'return call' to Max. He answered on the first ring.

"Hey babe, what's up?"

Josie took a deep breath, "I'll be your subbie, Max, on one condition though."

"Yeah, that's great babe! You won't regret this, Josie, I promise you! What's the condition? Cos' you know that subbies don't get to set conditions, right, li'l girl?" He growled softly.

"I know. Just this one thing, Max, I want us to take a trip to Denver this weekend, I want my grandparents to meet you."

The End

A Message from Vanessa Brooks

I hope that you have enjoyed reading *Twin Turmoil.* I like to write for my readers and the only way I can find out what you want from a book is when you leave a review. Please do take a moment of your time and leave your own review, thank you!

I always welcome comments from my readers. You can find me on:

Twitter: www.twitter.com/blushingvanessa
Or visit my web page: http://vanessanovels.wix.com/vanessanovels
Or e-mail me: vanessanovels@inbox.com

Vanessa Brooks

International bestselling author Vanessa Brooks lives in Sussex, England. She has a lifelong love of history, most especially English and American. She has written a few western tales, one notably for the Red Petticoat series, which was such a huge success in America. Her Georgian series, Masterful Husbands, set in the 1700's, also proved highly successful on both sides of the Atlantic

Vanessa's novels are generally historically based; she has a knack of bringing authenticity into the eras in which her novels are set. She carefully researches every time period, and strives to ensure that any historical facts she uses are correct.

More importantly, Vanessa likes writing entertaining books that her readers will enjoy. She includes passion, adventure, romance and domestic discipline – de rigueur within past times.

If you read it and enjoyed it, please leave a review!

Thank you!

Don't miss these exciting titles by Vanessa Brooks and Blushing Books!

Sunny's Safe Haven

Cowboy Caveat

Twin Turmoil

Corbin's Bend

Sub-Divided

A Shift in Time Series

Lightning Switch, Book 1
Wylde Switch, Book 2

Masterful Husbands Series
His Colonial Rose, Prequel
Sir Thomas's Bride, Book One
Viscount Weston's Bride, Book Two
The Colonel's Bride, Book Three
The Smuggler's Bride, Book Four
Masterful Husbands Tame Their Wives (Complete Series)

Victorian Melodramas Series
Elspeth, Book One
Amanda, Book Two
Victorian Rogues Compilation (Complete Series)

The Adventures of Linnett Wainwright
His Spoilt Lady, Book One
His Defiant Wife, Book Two
Her Match, Her Mate, Her Master, Complete Series

Anthologies
Historical Heroes
Sweet Town Love
12 Naughty Days of Christmas 2016

Audible Books
Sir Thomas's Bride
Viscount Weston's Bride
Cowboy Caveat
Sunny's Safe Haven

Connect with Vanessa Brooks:
vanessanovels.wix.com/vanessanovels

vanessanovels@inbox.com

Blushing Books

Blushing Books is one of the oldest eBook publishers on the web. We've been running websites that publish spanking and BDSM related romance and erotica since 1999, and we have been selling eBooks since 2003. We hope you'll check out our hundreds of offerings at http://www.blushingbooks.com.

Milton Keynes UK
Ingram Content Group UK Ltd.
UKHW011843080124
435686UK00001B/48

9 781645 631323